DEEP CHECK

KIMBERLY KINCAID

Enjoy!

Kim Kincaid

DEEP CHECK

© 2017 Kimberly Kincaid

❀ Created with Vellum

This book is dedicated to singer/songwriter Michael Ray,
whose song "Think A Little Less" inspired the love story,
and to singer/songwriter Matt Nathanson,
whose song "Adrenaline" inspired the (ahem) sexy bits.
Download their music responsibly, y'all!

ACKNOWLEDGMENTS

Although my name is on the cover of this book, it was far from a solitary endeavor. Huge, huge thanks to Nicole Bailey, for reading all the words (and fixing all the commas!) and Jaycee DeLorenzo, for the incredible cover art. You two are my dream team!

This project certainly never would have existed without Avery Flynn's evil genius and backbreaking effort. I'm so wildly grateful to have worked with you, Flynnie, along with Robin Covington (who did a lot of plotting—and re-plotting —of this book with me!), Desiree Holt, Heather Long, Nana Malone, Virginia Nelson, Xio Axelrod, Christi Barth, Andie J. Christopher, Kim Golden, Lena Hart, Robin Kaye, Katie Kenyhercz, Kate Meader, Angi Morgan, Susan Scott Shelley, and Misty D. Waters.

Profound gratitude, as always, to my family, who is so supportive of my quirky writing habits and my crazy schedule. I love you all more than words can express.

But my deepest thanks go out to you, the readers holding this book. Without your kind words on social media, your enthusiasm for my stories, your requests for more books, I could not do what I do. Thank you for reading Finn and January's story, and for being the most fierce, voracious, wonderful fandom out there. I love you all!

PROLOGUE

GAME SEVEN OF THE CUP FINALS. NEW ORLEANS
CAJUN RAGE: 1, NEW YORK SPARTANS: 0. SERIES TIED,
3-3. TWENTY SECONDS LEFT IN REGULATION.

Finnegan Donnelly needed a fucking miracle. And seeing as how the man upstairs had already dished one up tonight by way of the ridiculous shot-block that had saved their goalie's ass and—oh by the way—the Rage's chance at winning the Cup, Finn was damn near certain they wouldn't get another.

Which meant the next twenty seconds of his life were about to get as ugly as homemade sin.

Finn scanned the ice, forcing his breath to slow down as his instincts fired up. The Spartans would need to throw everything they had at the Rage's net if they wanted to tie this thing up and force overtime; hell, they were already in position to do just that. Shifting. Advancing. Bearing down.

No. No way was Finn going to let that happen. The Rage

was too close. *He* was too close, and the win was the only thing he'd wanted for the last seven years.

Okay, Ash. Help a brother out. Just twelve more seconds. Eleven. Ten...

Finn's muscles screamed beneath his pads, but he welcomed the pain. Lasering his focus on the Rage's goal, he rushed forward with only one purpose: defend. Their goalie and Finn's closest friend on the team, Flynn Kazakov, dropped into a menacing stance as every last player on both teams rushed forward. Skates hissed, scraping and slapping the ice, but Finn was oddly calm, focused. His heart pounded with each second—thump-*thump*, maneuver. Thump-*thump*, hold. Thump-*thump*, defend.

Thump-*thump*. Win.

The Spartan's center unleashed a punishing shot, aiming right for the space over Kazakov's shoulder, and Finn's composure slipped. Throwing everything he had into the movement, he raced toward the goal.

Two, one...

The puck clattered to the ice outside of the net, and holy shit. Holy *shit*. They'd done it.

They'd won the Cup.

Finn's heart catapulted against his rib cage, his breath jamming in his lungs for just a split second before releasing in an unholy shout. His teammates—bunch of scrappers and wanna-bes and has-beens that they were—swarmed the ice, all of them tackling each other and whooping and pumping their fists in the air. The keeper brought the Cup onto the ice and handed it over to Coach Thibodeault, who lifted it high overhead. But rather than skating over to join the melee, Finn dropped to his knees on the ice, letting his eyes squeeze shut.

Asher had always said, always *known* Finn would get here

one day. His best friend had been the only person who had believed Finn would fulfill his dream of winning it all.

And now, seven years after he'd wrecked their friendship and left Remington without a backward glance, he would go back to the hometown he hated with a passion in order to bring the Cup to Asher's grave.

CHAPTER 1

THREE WEEKS LATER

"If you're trying to kill me, I've got to admit, this is probably going to do the job."

January Sinclair sat back against the electric blue banquette of her favorite booth at the Fork in the Road diner and laughed despite the gravity of her father's words. "The whole point is that this *isn't* going to kill you," she said, gesturing to the breakfast on the Formica between them.

Her father's frown, however, didn't budge. "Oh yes it is. I'm going to die of boredom."

January looked at the pair of bran muffins, each with a side order of sliced bananas, and ugh, he had a point. "Look, I know this breakfast is a little bland, but between your cholesterol and your blood pressure, you've got to make some changes, Dad."

"I run an intelligence unit in the busiest police district in Remington," he said, the lift at the corners of his mouth certainly a sign of affection for his job rather than the thimble-sized cup of decaf he'd just liberated from the table. "High blood pressure is an occupational gold standard."

January's heart twisted beneath her light blue blouse, but she covered the sensation with a breezy smile. Yes, her father's workaholic lifestyle and his questionable eating habits were a big deal. But spotlighting that out loud wouldn't get her anywhere, so she simply said, "Not anymore. Here, have some tomato juice. It's loaded with vitamins."

"For the record, it's also awful." He raised one blond brow at her, his stare narrowing in the abundant June sunlight spilling in through the diner's windows. "Are you going to make me resort to my bad cop routine in order to get some bacon?"

"Well that depends."

"On?"

January dialed her voice to its gentlest setting, but didn't scale back on her words. "Whether or not you're going to make me remind you that I'm your only child as well as your only living family member, and that since Mom lives eight thousand miles away on an ashram in India and I haven't spoken to her in easily a year, you're pretty much my only family too. Which means I'd like to keep you around for as long as possible, if that's alright with you."

"Dammit," her father muttered, picking up the tomato juice and taking a sip. "You're tough as hell, you know that?"

January buried her smile in her coffee cup. "Thank you. I come by it honestly."

"So how are things at the firehouse?" her father asked, reluctantly spearing a slice of banana with his fork as he shifted the subject. "Those guys aren't working you too hard, I hope."

"First of all, some of those guys are women," she reminded him jokingly. Shae McCullough and Quinn

Copeland were just as much a part of Station Seventeen's A-shift as the engine and the ambulance they rode on.

Her father raised his hands in concession. "Figure of speech. Some of my best guys are women, too. Speaking of which, Moreno told me to tell you she says hello."

"Oooh, tell her I said hi back." Isabella Moreno might be one of her father's detectives, but she was also living with Kellan Walker, who just so happened to be a firefighter on A-shift. As far as January was concerned, that made Isabella part of the Seventeen family, too. "And secondly, I love my job at the firehouse. They're not working me too hard at all."

"You've been their administrator for almost four years," her father allowed. "You run a tight enough ship that even a mountain of work looks like a speed bump to you."

January took a bite of the bran muffin she'd ordered in solidarity and shrugged. "I don't mind working hard to keep things running smoothly over there. Those guys are my family, just like you."

"And I thought I was the workaholic." Her father gave up a wry twist of his lips, which she didn't think twice about returning.

"You are. I guess that's another thing I come by honestly."

"Is that why you're chairing next month's firehouse fundraiser?"

Her pulse stuttered in surprise. She'd just agreed to take the volunteer position yesterday. "Who told you that?"

"I'm a police sergeant." Her father tried on his most serious poker face. "I know things."

Ah. Of course. "Isabella ratted me out." January knew she shouldn't have said anything when they'd hung out at the Crooked Angel last night.

"She mentioned it when I talked to her this morning," he admitted. "But come on. Pulling together a fundraiser in four short weeks on top of your regular workload is a pretty big deal. Not to mention a pretty big undertaking, kid."

"Dad. I just turned twenty-five." Although she tried to keep her tone serious, she was pretty sure her laughter canceled out any admonition the protest at her nickname might've otherwise carried.

Her father wasn't having it, though, with or without the laughter. "And when you're ninety-five, you'll still be my kid. You worry about me, I worry about you. Now stop dodging the subject."

Ah, busted. "Who's tough now?" she groused. But her father crossed his arms over the front of his dark green button down shirt, and shit, he wasn't going to let her off the hook unless she convinced him to.

"You don't have to worry about me." She took another bite of her muffin. "This is what I went to college for, remember?"

Pride whisked through her father's eyes. "I remember."

January's cheeks warmed. Of course he did. He'd been in the third row when she'd graduated *summa cum laude* with her degree in marketing, for cripes' sake.

She threw back the last of her coffee, because it was less conspicuous than clearing her throat. "I know what I'm in for with planning a fundraiser on the fly. Anyway, I think they're fun."

One blond brow arched from across the table. "You think they're boring and pretentious."

"Okay. I think this one is going to be fun," she amended with a bigger than necessary smile. This fundraiser *would* be fun. Provided she could figure out something new and fresh (and okay, fast) to make it that way, anyhow.

"Well, I know it'll take a lot of work, but if anyone can plan a successful event, it's you," her father said.

Just like that, January's smile became a whole lot less forced. "I really hope so."

Planning this fundraiser was likely to make her month pretty crazy, but the money raised would go toward new, state-of-the-art equipment for the firefighters. Busting her buns for four weeks seemed like a small price to pay. She knew all too well how much steeper the price could be.

God, she missed Asher. She missed her best friend.

She'd miss Finn too, if she wasn't so pissed at him.

January tamped down the thought even as it sent a pang through her belly. Finn had made his choices. Found the success he'd wanted. Left her behind in the process.

She needed to leave him behind too. No matter how badly she'd wanted him when he left Remington seven years ago.

Fundraiser. Equipment. Firehouse. Immediately, if not sooner.

"Right!" January said, just a second too quickly and a shade too loud. Tugging in a breath, she made sure to meter the rest of her words to match her smile. "Well, I hate to eat and run, but I have to be at work in fifteen minutes, and today's going to be busy."

She reached into her purse to cover her half of breakfast, but her father stopped her with a wave of his hand.

"Go." He slid out of the booth to give her a quick hug. "Let me know if the Thirty-Third can help with the fundraiser."

She brushed a kiss over her father's cheek. "Thanks, I will. And Dad?" She waited for him to make full eye contact before continuing. "Do me a favor and wait until I'm out of the parking lot to order that side of bacon, okay?"

He laughed in a full admission of guilt. "I'll finish the juice if that makes you feel any better."

"Actually, it does," she said, giving up a grin along with one last wave as she headed for the chrome and glass double doors.

∽

FINN SAT BACK against the well-cushioned seat in the Lincoln Town Car that had picked him up at the airport, wishing like hell the thing had a mini bar. He'd have been more than happy to simply rent a car and drive himself, but his twenty-four hours with the Cup started bright and early tomorrow morning, which meant not only did he have to travel with it in its gigantic protective trunk, but with the keeper of the Cup as well.

Talk about surreal. Once upon a time, his primary address had been the backseat of a beat-to-hell-and-back Chevy, and now, Finn had a fucking entourage.

"Alrighty!" The keeper of the Cup, Edwin Motz, clambered into the passenger seat of the Town Car and turned to give Finn a double thumbs-up. "The Cup is all strapped in and secure in the van behind us, so we're good to go. Sorry it took a minute, but I had to double-triple check to make sure it arrived without a scratch."

Unable to help himself, Finn lifted one corner of his mouth in an expression caught somewhere between a smile and a smirk. "The Cup never left its trunk, Edwin. A trunk that's custom-padded and insulated and probably bulletproof on top of that."

"Oh, a bulletproof trunk. That *would* be a good idea," Edwin said, his eyes going wide behind the thick, dark rims of his glasses. "Imagine how well-protected the Cup would stay if we—"

Finn interrupted by turning his smirk into a laugh. "I was actually kidding about the bulletproof thing."

"Oh. Right, right, of course." Edwin nodded, but tapped out a quick note on his iPhone that made Finn think a bid for a bulletproof trunk might be in the Cup's future. "At any rate, you're the first player with the Cup this year. The Rage's win is only a few weeks old, so we'll probably get a little more press than usual."

Finn brought his teeth together, biting back the urge to tell Edwin they wouldn't be getting any press at all. His agent had practically had a kitten—Finn *was* hip deep in contract negotiations. But all that smile-for-the-camera press Marty wanted would have to wait until after Finn had gone to Asher's grave. After he'd righted the wrong that had wedged between them for far too long.

After he'd tied up all his loose ends and gotten the fuck out of Remington, once and for all.

"Did you need me to go over any of the rules with you before tomorrow?" Edwin turned to rummage through the bag on his lap, presumably for a fresh copy of the six-page spreadsheet he'd already given all the players on the care and keeping of the Cup, but Finn shook his head to stop the guy mid-move.

"Your handout was pretty clear," he said, watching the buildings and storefronts of downtown Remington flash by as the driver maneuvered through rush hour traffic. Christ, so much had changed in the last seven years. Including him, he supposed.

Hell if *that* wasn't the whole point of this trip.

Finn took a deep inhale and rerouted his attention back to Edwin to count off the highlights. "Nothing illegal. Nothing that will damage the Cup. No charging anyone for photo ops with the Cup." That one had surprised him, actually. He wasn't exactly a saint (or, you know, even fucking close) but you had to be a special breed of dickhead to go there. "Hey, do guys seriously try to do that?"

"I think you'd be shocked to know what some people try to do with it," Edwin replied gravely, and ooookay. Moving on.

"And the number one rule of my day with the Cup is I can take it anywhere I want as long as it never leaves your sight."

Edwin nodded, pushing his glasses higher over the bridge of his nose. "That about sums things up, yes. If you've got an itinerary for tomorrow, I can make a detailed plan to help you deal with the press accordingly."

"I don't."

"I'm sorry." Confusion pulled the edges of the keeper's mouth into a frown. "I thought…well, the dossier you have on file with the Rage says you lived here in Remington for five years before you went to the minors in Tallahassee. Since it doesn't list anything before that, I assumed this was your hometown."

Finn made a mental note to have his team dossier shredded into confetti as soon as he got back to New Orleans. Not that anyone other than Edwin actually read those goddamn things. "It's not."

"Oh." Edwin's fingers twitched over the seat back, and Finn would bet the bank the guy was just itching to go in and edit Finn's personnel file right there from the front seat of the Town Car. "Well then, perhaps just a list of places you'd like to go so I can call ahead to make arrangements," Edwin tried again. "It really *is* in your best interest to be prepared for your day with the Cup so there are no mishaps."

"There won't be any mishaps." Finn directed his gaze out the window again, hoping the move would put a cap on the conversation.

No such luck. Not that luck had ever been in Finn's wheelhouse. "Mr. Donnelly, I really think we should—"

"I'm all set, Edwin."

A tiny part of Finn felt bad for killing the conversation so abruptly. But the guys on the team—Kazakov, Ford Callaghan, James "DC" Washington; hell, every last one of those crazy sons of bitches—*they* were the only close friends

Finn had, and they'd each get their own day with the Cup. He didn't have any grand plans. No local parade, no rah rah fanfare. No family members to oooh and aaah over the thing.

The only place he wanted to take it was Asher's grave so he could finally make amends for the way he'd busted up their friendship, the way he damn well should have before Asher had died.

But Ash isn't the only best friend you burned a bridge with here in Remington, now is he?

The thought came out of nowhere, hitting Finn like a slap shot at center mass. Edwin had smartly turned his attention to their driver, regaling the poor guy with one hockey statistic after another, so Finn gave in to the weird urge to go all blast from the past and slide deeper into his thoughts.

He should've known January would edge her way into his brain pan as soon as he set foot in Remington. After all, he and Asher and January had been best friends from the beginning of the eighth grade to the day they'd graduated high school. She'd been bright and kind and funny as hell, the polar opposite of Finn's gruff attitude and shitty upbringing.

She'd been a perfect match for Asher, though. Which was actually pretty fitting, seeing as how the guy had been in love with her since the day he'd clapped eyes on her. Not that Finn could blame him. Even in high school, January had been a fucking knockout, with those ice-blue eyes that crinkled around the edges when she laughed and that dusting of freckles over the bridge of her nose that she'd hated, but Finn had always secretly thought were sexy.

God love Asher and his titanium sense of honor, though. He'd never worked up the nerve to risk turning his friendship with January into anything more. Or hell, maybe he had, after the night everything had gone to shit between the three of them.

Jamming a hand through his hair, Finn shoved his

thoughts back down where they belonged. The past was behind him for a reason, just as he'd left Remington for a reason. Yeah, his friendship with January had ended as a consequence, and yeah again, he missed her hard, more than he'd usually admit.

But he couldn't go back. Not to the friendship he'd never deserved, even though she'd given it so fast and so freely. Not to the dilapidated house his father had left him two years ago when the old man had died. Not to the shitty reality of who he'd been and how he'd been raised—or more to the point, *not* raised by the man when his mother had pulled her disappearing act.

No, Finn most definitely couldn't go back. But there was one thing he *could* do.

As soon as he and Edwin and the Cup were checked in all safe and secure at the Remington Plaza hotel, he could go find that drink he was beginning to desperately need.

~

FINN TIPPED his head to take in the sign reading *The Crooked Angel Bar and Grille*, and good Christ, this was more like it. After sitting at the bar in the lobby of the Plaza for a solid half an hour, all he'd gotten was an under-poured glass of whiskey and an overwhelming case of hives. His suite, with its panoramic view of the city and its fully stocked gourmet kitchen and its bathtub big enough for him and half his teammates, was definitely kickass. But all the chi-chi old money business that went with a hotel like the Plaza?

No fucking thank you. A cold bottle of beer and the corner bar stool were so much more Finn's speed.

Tugging the front door open, he spun a gaze around the inside of the Crooked Angel. The place was pretty crowded, although considering the two-sided chalkboard sign

"Shouldn't I be asking you the same thing?" Finn volleyed. "I thought you worked at the firehouse."

Her lips parted, betraying her surprise. But just because he hadn't spoken to her at Asher's funeral didn't mean he hadn't seen her with the firefighters who had laid their brother to rest, or overheard them talking about her administrative position at Station Seventeen.

She didn't give him an inch, though. "And I thought you lived in New Orleans."

"I'm in town for a few days. Figured a drink wouldn't be so bad," he said, lowering his gaze to the beer in her hand so he wouldn't stare at her instead. Christ, she looked fucking gorgeous. He shouldn't be surprised, he guessed. She'd been gorgeous since the day he'd met her on Asher's front porch over a decade ago, all honey-colored hair and huge-hearted disposition and sweet, sexy smiles. "And for the record, no one calls me by my full name but you."

"Well that's interesting," she said, her gold-blond brows arching slightly as she plucked a cocktail napkin from the plastic dispenser to her left and placed his beer on the bar in front of him. "Since I don't call you at all."

Finn bit down on the urge to wince. Not that he didn't deserve the direct hit, but… "No. I guess you don't."

Silence settled between them, thick and tightly strung, until finally, January shocked the hell out of him with, "Congratulations on winning the Cup. I know it's what you wanted."

"Thanks. I did." Whether it was the fresh emotion of seeing her after so long or the old emotion of being back in Remington, Finn had no clue. But something twisted in his chest, prompting his mouth open without his brain's permission. "Listen, I know I—"

"Christ on a Pop-Tart, Sinclair! Do you know whose beer you just poured?"

Finn blinked at the tall, dark-haired guy standing beside him, his knee-jerk frustration at the interruption quickly chased off by relief. Had he seriously been T-minus two seconds from blabbing to January—of *all* goddamn people— why he'd come back to Remington?

"I used to," she murmured, so softly that Finn barely caught the words before she pasted an over-bright smile onto her lips. "Mmm hmm! Kellan Walker, meet Finn Donnelly. Kellan's a firefighter at Station Seventeen," she told him, her cheeks flushing just enough to trip Finn's oh-fuck-yes trigger before she turned her attention back to the guy, adding, "And Finn is…obviously Finn. We used to know each other back in high school."

"Ah, that's right," Kellan said, extending his hand toward Finn for a firm shake. "I'm a Remington transplant, so I've only been here for three years. But I'd heard you were from the area. Congrats on winning the Cup, man. We were rooting for the Rage all the way."

"Thanks. I appreciate that."

Finn shifted his gaze back to the spot where January stood behind the bar, smiling at Kellan as she twisted the lid from a fresh bottle of beer before exchanging it for his empty one. An unwanted thought flared to life in his brain, followed by a stab of something hot and ugly he couldn't quite identify. "So you two know each other from the firehouse?"

"Yeah." Kellan passed over a few bills, tipping January well, and dammit, Finn actually liked the guy. "Well, that and January's old man is my girlfriend's sergeant over at the Thirty-Third. So I guess you could say we're one big convoluted family."

Just like that, Finn's affection for the guy tripled. "I've got one of those myself. If you count a bunch of smelly lunatics who also just so happen to know their way around the ice."

"Sounds like firehouses have a lot in common with

hockey teams. Speaking of which"—Kellan's face lit with a genuinely friendly smile that made Finn understand why Asher had wanted to be a firefighter so much—"a bunch of us from Seventeen are over at our regular tables. If you're hanging out solo, you're welcome to join us."

Finn's gaze took an involuntary trip to January, which prompted Kellan's to do the same before he tacked on a quick, "Unless you two are catching up."

"No. We're not."

Although Finn had expected January's reply, it still hit him right in the solar plexus. But he couldn't make up for the last seven years in a night. Hell, even though he'd had damn good reasons for cutting her out of his life so abruptly, Finn couldn't make up for the last seven years *ever*.

The damage between them was done. He'd been the one to do it. So now he had no choice but to say, "It was really good to see you again, Calendar Girl. Have a nice night," before sliding a twenty across the glossy wood of the bar and walking away.

CHAPTER 2

January methodically filled three more drink orders before she remembered how to breathe. But come on—the last time she'd seen Finn had been at Asher's funeral, where he'd steadfastly ignored her presence, and the time before that, he'd crushed her feelings into dust. Now he was here in her favorite hangout like it was no big deal, calling her by that silly nickname only he used and looking hot enough to require a legal disclaimer stamped across his freaking forehead?

On second thought, maybe she hadn't remembered how to breathe just yet.

"Whoa." Kennedy's olive green eyes widened beneath the heavy fringe of her bangs as she looked up from the row of tequila shots she'd just poured. "Are you okay?"

"Yep. I'm great." The answer shoveled out of January's mouth by default, probably much the same as Kennedy's snort in response, and *dammit*. Her friend was as street savvy as she was sharp-eyed. January wasn't going to get away with anything less than full disclosure.

She adjusted the dark red half-apron knotted over her

jeans before helping Kennedy arrange the shot glasses onto a tray in a precise row. "You didn't tell me the hot IPA guy at the end of the bar was Finn Donnelly." She waited out her friend's apologetic ooookay-style pause for a beat, then two before adding, "He plays center for the Cajun Rage. They won the Cup a few weeks ago. We had all seven playoff games on every screen in the bar."

"Ah, hockey. Well, that explains the ridiculous muscles," Kennedy said, turning to hand off the tray full of bad ideas to a passing waitress. "I take it you know the guy."

Hello, gargantuan understatement. But since January couldn't exactly come off with *if by 'know him' you mean 'truly, desperately, deeply lusted after him all the way through high school until he shot me down cold, had a huge blowout fight with our other best friend, then went completely radio silent even when said best friend suddenly died in the line of duty' then yes, I know the shit out of Finn Donnelly*, she went with, "What makes you think that?"

"Aside from the fact that he's looked over here three times in as many minutes and your cheeks are doing a fabulous impression of a five-alarm fire, you mean?" Kennedy asked, and January's laugh in reply was as soft as it was humorless.

"Believe me, he's not looking over here. And yes, Finn and I went to high school together, so I, um, used to know him."

One corner of Kennedy's merlot-colored mouth kicked up into a smirk as she dropped her voice to a volume too quiet for any of the nearby patrons to hear. "Are we talking like, you knew him in passing, you'd say 'hi, how's it going' on the way to algebra, or did you *know* him-know him, like vaginally?"

Heat shot down January's spine at the thought of Finn anywhere near her girly bits, and God, so much for her cheeks getting back to a passably normal color. "Neither, actually."

"Really?" Kennedy opened one of the glass-topped coolers built in beneath the bar, popping the tops of two bottles of Budweiser for the couple to her left. "This guy—Finn, right? He might not be my type, but I didn't call him Hot IPA Guy because he looked like he was running a fever. Between that dark, curly hair and that bad-boy smile he's got going on, he's pretty lickable, and like it or not, your blush *is* giving you away. You two seriously never hooked up?"

She and Finn in the kitchen at his going away party...impulsively kissing him after one beer too many...the hot, hungry slide of his mouth on hers as—just for a breath—he'd pulled her against the hard length of his body and kissed her back...

January swiped a dish towel over the bar even though the glossy stretch of wood in front of her was already spotless. "No. Finn definitely doesn't see me as hookup material. He and I used to be best friends." She cleared her throat before adding, "With Asher."

"Asher Gibson?" In an instant, Kennedy's expression lost its sassy edge. She might not have been raised in Remington like a lot of their crowd, but she'd been around everyone from Station Seventeen long enough to have known exactly who Asher was. Along with what had happened to him. "I didn't know you two were that close."

January's heart squeezed. They had been close. Right up until the night she'd kissed Finn, and then... "It's kind of a long story," she said, turning to rearrange the boxes of straws and cocktail napkins beneath the bar.

"I'm sorry." Kennedy's tone, usually full of brass and devoid of bullshit, was shockingly soft. "I didn't mean to push a sore subject."

Scooping in a deep breath, January shook her head. Asher would've been pissed purple at anyone tiptoeing around his memory, and anyway, the debacle with Finn was in the past.

Just because he was sitting halfway across the bar instead of halfway across the country didn't change that.

"It's really more of a closed subject. At least where Finn is concerned."

January paused to fill a few drink orders and deliver a plate of hot wings to a pair of women sitting at the bar. Although Kennedy had kept equally busy, January could feel the questions still brewing in her stare, and when they finally had a lull, she nodded Kennedy over to the small service alcove by the cash register, blowing out a breath in defeat.

"When I was in the eighth grade, my dad and I moved in next door to the Gibsons. Asher and I became friends, and he already knew Finn from this hockey league they played in together. The three of us were pretty much Epoxied at the hip all through high school."

Unable to help it, her gaze moved over the crowded bar to zero in on Finn, and God, wasn't hockey supposed to be *hard* on a guy's face?

"Anyway." She snapped her attention back over to the alcove, rearranging the clean pint glasses stacked on one of the low shelves. "After the three of us graduated, Asher and I went to Remington University, but Finn left town so he could play minor league hockey. He was always really good, and working his way up the ranks to win the Cup was the only thing he ever wanted."

Kennedy—being Kennedy—didn't skip so much as a fraction of a beat. "Is that why you're not tight anymore? Because he left to play hockey?"

"No."

"No?" Kennedy's dark brows shot upward, and ugh, better to just go the Band-Aid route even though January knew damn well saying everything out loud would sting.

"No. We're not friends anymore because I kissed him like

a lovesick idiot at his going away party. Asher walked in on us, and the two of them got into a fistfight."

"Wait. Were you and Asher…" Kennedy trailed off, but January filled in the blanks easily enough.

"Oh God, no." She punctuated the words with a shake of her head. "Don't get me wrong, I loved the guy, but I always looked at him like a brother. I suspected once or twice that he might want more than friendship," she admitted. "Which he clearly did, since he and Finn got into it that night over the kiss. But Asher had never said anything about it to me before the fight."

"And you'd had a thing for Finn the whole time," Kennedy said, and even though she was simply stating the obvious, January's pride let out a healthy squall.

"Stupidly, as it turned out. After he and Asher went all cage match on each other, Finn told me he was just drunk, the kiss had been a huge mistake"—January paused to let Kennedy mutter a few top shelf swear words in Finn's honor —"then he left town the next day, and I never heard from him again. Asher and I stayed friends, but not like we had been. We never talked about his feelings for me, and we definitely never talked about Finn. The whole thing ended in a pretty big mess."

"What about when Asher died in that house fire? You and Finn didn't even talk then?" Disbelief colored Kennedy's voice, her forehead creasing to match, but the answer to this one was sadly just as straightforward as the rest.

"Nope. He came back to Remington for the funeral, but he avoided me like a virus outbreak and left directly afterward."

Leaning a jeans-clad hip against the counter, Kennedy sent a furtive glance toward Station Seventeen's usual pair of tables, her expression growing thoughtful. "So now he's just back out of the blue?"

"For a few days, I guess," January said, turning to grab a double order of nachos from the kitchen pass and get on with her night, once and for all. "But I'm sure he'll blaze a fast path out of town as soon as he's able. He's pretty good at leaving."

"Sounds like you've got a lot of history, though. You're sure you don't want to air things out with him before he goes?"

The question alone took January by surprise. The "no" burning in her mouth, just begging to be said in reply?

Shocked her enough to make her hands shake.

Don't be stupid, she chided, squaring her shoulders beneath the dark blue cotton of her tank top. "Yes. I'm sure."

She might've had feelings for Finn once, and God knew there had been moments—especially after Asher had died—when she'd have given damn near anything for the chance to talk to him again. But those moments were behind her. *Finn* was behind her.

The best thing January could do now was to leave him there and keep moving on.

~

Finn stared at the ceiling, trying like fuck to reconcile the irony of being surrounded by the priciest bed sheets in all of Remington and not being able to sleep so much as a wink. But between the gut-twisting thought of going to the cemetery later today and his unexpected run-in with January last night, being able to restfully close his eyes was a definite no-go.

Especially since every time he'd tried, all he could see were the subtle yet sexy changes January had grown into over the last seven years. The flawless press of her ass against those jeans that surrendered to her curves in all the best places. The slide of her ponytail over one slim shoulder when she leaned in to place a drink on the bar. The way her heart-shaped lips gave way to a surprisingly throaty laugh every time one of her friends from Station Seventeen went over to say hello and grab another drink.

Christ, those lips. How anything that looked so sweet could feel so sinful, Finn had no idea. But in seven goddamn years, he'd never been as turned on by a kiss as he'd been by January's, so brash and yet so full of need. He'd wanted a month with her mouth alone, to coax filthy words past those pretty lips, to feel them wrapped around his cock as she did the same to him...

Heat flared to life between his legs, making his dick stir beneath the thin material of his basketball shorts, but oh no. *Hell* no. He didn't care how hot her laugh (or her mouth...or that sweet spot where her leg met the curve of her ass...or even that adorable little furrow that built between her eyebrows whenever she looked over a drink ticket) was.

January wasn't for him. She never had been, no matter how much he'd secretly wished otherwise. Which meant he needed to start thinking with his upstairs head and *stop* thinking about January's ass.

Damn, he was a terrible friend.

Grating out a curse, Finn looked at the clock on his bedside table. He wasn't a total stranger to four thirty a.m., what with his whole mantra of I-practice-while-everyone-else-sleeps. But he hadn't scratched his way through the minors on his good looks, and he sure as shit hadn't made the Rage on anything less than a mountain of ass-busting work.

Reaching for the iPad he'd left next to the alarm clock, he tapped the screen to life, diving headfirst into game film. The highlights kept Finn mostly occupied until the sun made an appearance at the edges of the electronic blinds covering the windows of his suite, at which point he threw back the four-inch thick bed covers and headed for the shower. He'd come back to Remington to take the Cup to Asher's grave, to finally make the amends that would let him move on for good. Waiting now seemed stupid.

Or at least, it did until he got to Remington Cemetery, at which point waiting seemed like a spectacular fucking plan.

Finn stared at the manicured grass and the neatly ordered headstones, unease forming a hard ball in his gut. He'd burned so much blood, sweat, and energy trying to *get* to this moment that he hadn't really thought about what he'd say once he'd actually arrived. He did, however, know who he wasn't going to say any of it in front of, so he knotted his arms over the center of his T-shirt and slid a glance at the roadside spot where Edwin stood next to him.

"I'm going to need some privacy," Finn said, unyielding, and to his surprise, the keeper nodded.

"Right, right. I mean, as you know, I have to be able to see the Cup at all times, and of course I do prefer to be as close as possible to ensure its utmost safety, but..." He trailed off, pushing his thickly framed glasses higher on the bridge of his nose as he cleared his throat. "Since this is clearly a personal matter, I'll just wait right over there on that bench. Would you, ah, like any help moving the Cup to a specific plot? It's deceptively heavy, and—"

"I'm good." Finn hated cutting the guy off. Hell, he hated everything about his current situation. But he couldn't have what he really wanted, and this was as close as he was going to get.

This was the only way he could talk to his best friend.

His muscles tightened and squeezed as he bent down and lifted the Cup from its case in the back of the SUV he'd broken down and had the car rental place drop off at the hotel so he could do his own driving. Hefting the thing to one hip, Finn walked a path toward Asher's grave, his work boots shushing over the dew-damp grass and his pulse knocking faster with every step.

Oh shit. He arrived at the tidily kept plot with his heart wedged in his throat. Forcing himself to focus, Finn looked down at the marker with Asher's name, birth date, and the day he'd died inscribed in the stone, letting go of a shaky breath.

"Hey, Ash." He shifted his weight beneath the heft of the Cup, sweat forming between his shoulder blades even though the morning sunlight hadn't yet jacked the temperature past the low seventies. "It's me. Finn. I'm sure you're, uh, probably surprised to see me here. And still a little pissed off, too."

He paused, the memory of the last words they'd ever spoken to each other spearing through his memory, and screw this. Finn had come here to make amends. He owed the guy this conversation, no matter how weird it felt that the talk was one-sided.

"Listen, I know I acted like a jackass seven years ago. I didn't mean for any of what happened to shake out the way it did. Which isn't an excuse," he said, because even though Asher had taken that first swing after he'd seen Finn and January kissing, Finn had swung back, and swung hard. "I just...I handled everything really badly. I didn't see that at the time, but after you died, I realized what a total shit I'd been, only then it was too late."

He looked down, fighting the emotion welling in his chest. "Anyway, you always believed in me, and you were a good friend, even when I wasn't. So I just came to say I'm sorry, and to, you know. Thank you for pushing me to never give up on my dreams. I know it doesn't make what happened between us any better, but I brought you this." Finn took a breath. Let it out along with three years' worth of want and hard work. "I finally won the Cup, like you always said I would."

Quiet settled in around him, punctuated by the occasional chirp of a bird and the low, steady drone of a lawn mower somewhere in the distance. He tried like hell to rummage up something else to say, but the harder he tried, the more awkward it felt to be standing here, yap-yapping to himself.

His stomach pitched, his shoulders beginning to ache from holding up thirty-five pounds of silver and nickel. He thought he'd feel closure—or at the very least, a budge in the heaviness that had been sitting so squarely on his shoulders ever since Asher had died. Somehow, though, this whole thing just felt clumsy and wrong, as if he'd managed to fuck things up even worse by coming here.

Jesus, he'd been an idiot to return to Remington. Asher was gone. January hated him. Bringing the Cup to Asher's grave wouldn't change that. Nothing would.

Finn turned on one heel with every intention of getting the hell out of this cemetery and the entire state of North Carolina. But a flash of bright yellow caught his eye from behind Asher's gravestone, his feet carrying him closer before his brain even registered the command to move. For a second that might have been a minute or a week or a goddamn eternity for all Finn knew, he stared at the bundle of flowers that had fallen behind the heavy gray slab. The surrounding plots were unmarked, signaling their emptiness, but even if they hadn't been, Finn would've known the flowers belonged to Asher.

They were lilies. January's favorite. Identical to the ones she'd placed on Asher's casket right after the firefighters from Station Seventeen had lowered him into the ground.

Finn's palms went slick against the base of the Cup, and he knelt down to place it in the grass before reaching for the flowers, the paper crinkling as he scooped them up for a closer inspection. The blooms were double-wrapped in tissue paper for added protection, the stems stuck into those plastic tubes of water that made the flowers last longer, and Finn's heart kicked hard against his ribs.

No one else would take such care with a simple bunch of flowers. But January had, just as she'd taken the time to care about Finn in high school even though he'd been an epic fuck-up, and oh *hell*.

Asher wasn't the only person he owed an apology to.

Placing the lilies carefully at the foot of the gravestone in front of him, Finn steadied both his hands and his resolve. Finding his feet, he lifted the Cup, and by the time he reached the SUV, his plan was one hundred percent solid.

"Where to now?" Edwin asked, arriving at Finn's side.

"Actually, I'd like to take the Cup someplace a little unconventional." At Edwin's look of sheer panic, Finn added, "Don't worry, I promise not to do anything crazy."

At least, he wouldn't do anything crazy with the Cup. As for the rest of his plan?

That had surpassed crazy before he'd even pushed up from the grass.

CHAPTER 3

J anuary looked at the stacks of paperwork covering every last inch of her desk and wondered if it was too early to drink. But since the time stamp on her computer monitor read ten forty-six a.m. and the piles were only bound to get bigger as the day went on, drowning her sorrows (or in this case, her planning for the annual Remington Fire Department fundraiser) wasn't really an option.

Anyway, if she was going to raise a glass to try and forget something, it would be the sinful, sexy smile of a certain hockey player she hadn't been able to get out of her mind for the last fourteen hours.

Straight.

"Oh, get to work," January muttered, swiping an over-stuffed folder off the tower of paperwork closest to her and propping it open. In a stroke of pure dumb luck, the thing held a week's worth of incident reports that Captain Bridges, a.k.a. her boss and the man in charge of Station Seventeen's entire A-shift, had just signed off on. Delivering the copies to Lieutenant Gamble on engine would take about thirty seconds, and more importantly, it would free up some exceedingly valuable real estate on her desk.

Pushing out of her chair, January tucked the folder in the crook of her arm and headed down the corridor toward the bunk room and lieutenants' offices, but the steady rhythm of her black patent leather heels clattered to a halt on the linoleum as she got halfway past the open entryway to the firehouse's common room.

And found herself staring at the most desired item in all of hockeydom.

"Is that…?" January struggled to get a coherent thought past all the *whaaaa?* winging around in her gray matter. But truly, she was just as likely to breeze past a herd of purple spotted elephants as she was the freaking Cup. No way was she seeing properly.

"Affirmative!" Kellan called out, waving her all the way past the threshold and into the crowded common room. "I know that filing system of yours keeps us all in line, but you've got to take a break to come see this. We have the Cup, right here in our firehouse! Isn't it *cool?*"

He flashed her a grin that spanned from ear to ear as he gestured to the spot where the Cup stood proudly on the dining table in the center of the room, surrounded by a throng of highly enthusiastic firefighters and paramedics and —good gravy, even Captain Bridges was standing beside the thing with a big ol' smile on his face. Just as it occurred to January that Finn must certainly be somewhere in the horde of people, the piercing sound of the all-call sounded off on the overhead speakers, sending a hush over the room.

"Engine Seventeen, Squad Six, Ambulance Twenty-Two, Battalion Seventeen, structure fire, forty-nine twelve Patterson Avenue, no reported entrapment. Requesting immediate response."

Instantly, the excitement vanished from the room, replaced by serious faces and clipped movements.

"Alright, people. Let's go." Captain Bridges jerked his chin toward the set of double doors leading out to the engine bay. "January," he said, his eyes landing on hers even though he was already in motion toward the exit. "Can you take care of our guests while we're out on this call, please?"

"Of course, Captain Bridges," she said, her heart clenching the same way it did every single time the all-call went off. "Be safe."

"Copy that," Bridges replied over his shoulder before disappearing briskly through the doors.

January pulled in a breath, bracing herself to face the only person who could be left in the room. Of the hundreds of thousands of people who threw on jeans and a T-shirt every day, how come Finn had to be the freaking sexiest one in the batch?

She didn't even want to get started on what he'd look like throwing *off* those clothes. Corded shoulders. Hard, flat pecs. Muscle-packed abs leading down to lean hips leading even lower to—

"That was a little intense," he said, tilting his head in the firefighters' wake, and the words brought January back to reality with a snap. Was she crazy? She'd promised Captain Bridges she'd be hospitable, not horny.

She put on her most polite expression and paired it with a crisp nod, even though a twinge of residual heat still lingered between her legs. "Getting out the door on the fire calls always is. That's what they're trained for, though, and they're very good at their jobs. They'll be okay." She had to believe that, because if she didn't... "So what are you doing here, anyway?"

One corner of Finn's mouth lifted with the suggestion of a smile. "That's the second time you've asked me that question in the last twenty-four hours, you know."

"This is the second time you've turned up in my path

unexpectedly," she pointed out, and his laughter in response rumbled a path up her spine.

"Fair enough. Every player on the Cup-winning team gets to spend a day with it, and today's my day. After hanging out with these guys last night, I thought maybe they'd get a kick out of me bringing the Cup here so they could see it up close."

Surprise mingled with something else January couldn't quite pin with a name. "You didn't want to stay in New Orleans with it?"

"No, I…" Finn paused, but only for a breath before shaking his head. "No."

A throat cleared from behind her, and January whipped around, her pulse popping in her veins.

"This is Edwin," Finn said, gesturing to the bespectacled man belonging to the not-quite-subtle interruption. "He's the keeper of the Cup. Here to make sure I don't lose it in a poker game or let it get run over by a semi or stolen by a band of bitter Spartans fans. That sort of thing."

Her lips parted. "People have tried to bet the Cup in poker games?"

Edwin answered before Finn could. "No. Of course not. Well, not since I've been the keeper, anyway. The Cup's safety and integrity is my utmost priority."

"I see." January shifted the folder she'd forgotten she was holding to the crook of her left arm in order to offer Edwin a handshake. "I'm January Sinclair, and I run the administrative side of the firehouse. It's nice to meet you."

"Likewise," he said, although his stiff nod didn't quite match the sentiment.

Annnnd cue her exit. "Well, you're both welcome to make yourselves at home here in the common room while you wait for the firefighters and paramedics to get back. There's fresh coffee, and we've got a handful of photo albums on the bookshelf here of some of our more memorable calls. If I catch an ETA over the radio, I'll be sure to update you."

But rather than stepping back to let her pass, Finn moved closer. "What about a tour?"

Surprise pushed her brows all the way up. "You want to haul the Cup on a tour of the firehouse?"

"No. I mean, not exactly. I'd like a tour of the firehouse, but Edwin can keep an eye on the Cup in here."

"Let me get this straight," she said slowly. "You've got the Cup for one day and one day only, and you want to leave it here in the common room while I take you on a look-see through the station?"

Edwin mirrored the doubtful frown January had worked up for the occasion, but Finn met both expressions with an unfaltering nod.

"Yes. That's exactly what I want."

"Why?"

Finn's whiskey-brown eyes flickered with emotion for a split second before he turned to look at Edwin in a clear bid for privacy. The other man scowled slightly, although he obliged with a muttered, "Fine. I'll just do a bit of reading, then," taking one of the house scrapbooks off the bookshelf and moving across the room.

As soon as he was out of earshot, Finn said, "I want a tour because I didn't just come here to see the firefighters and paramedics. I came here to see you. I was hoping we could talk."

"You're a little late for a talk, don't you think?"

The words slipped out before January could check them, but he surprised her by nodding in agreement.

"Actually, I do." Finn looked at her, swiping a hand through his already-tousled dark brown hair before running his palm over the back of his neck. "I know this is way, way overdue, and if you want to tell me to fuck off, well, I can't say I wouldn't understand. But I owe you an apology. A really big one, in fact, and I..."

He broke off, his gaze dropping to the floor. A thousand thoughts whipped through January's mind, urging her to give them voice. But before she could choose between asking him why now, admitting how ridiculously much she'd missed him, and—okay, yeah—launching the 'fuck off' he really did deserve, Finn stepped toward the door.

"You know what, this was a bad idea. I blindsided you at work, and that's a really uncool thing to do, so I'm just going to—"

"Was it a mistake?"

"What?" He looked at her, absolutely stunned, which was great, because that made two of them. But despite her graceless delivery, January needed to know the truth.

"You just said coming here was a bad idea"—she paused for a stabilizing breath before adding—"but bad ideas aren't always the same as mistakes. So what I want to know is, do you think coming here was a mistake?"

For the longest time, Finn did nothing but look at her with an expression she couldn't decipher on a dare. Then, holding on to her gaze, he crossed the linoleum until they were separated by less than an arm's length as he said, "I regret a lot of things, Calendar Girl, but coming here to apologize to you isn't one of them."

January's heart thrummed against her rib cage, and she hugged the folder to the front of her sheer white button-down in an effort to calm it, or at the very least, cover the stupid thing up. Finn had acted like a jackass, and no amount of apologizing could change that. He'd hurt her. He'd shut down their friendship without a word. Now here he was, standing in front of her with that light brown stare that could melt her like snow in a soft rain and the gruff, serious demeanor that had kept him tough all through high school, asking for the talk she'd wanted for the past seven years.

And she had to decide whether or not to give it to him.

A minute stretched into two, and January stood rooted to the floor tiles, until finally, she made up her mind all at once.

"Thank you for your honesty, Finnegan." Straightening her shoulders, she pivoted toward the door, covering more than half the distance to the exit before turning to look at him over her shoulder. "Well? Are you coming or not?"

"Holy shit. I mean"—Finn cleared his throat, clearly shocked as hell that she'd said yes. Which sort of made two of them—"Yes. I'm...yes."

He swung a quick glance at Edwin, who—other than sitting close enough to the Cup that he might as well be surgically attached—seemed to be fairly well occupied with the photo album he'd picked up. Finn didn't seem troubled in the least to leave the Cup in favor of talking to her, though, readily following her through the open entryway leading to Station Seventeen's front lobby. Not really sure what to say now that she'd agreed to hear him out, January stuck to what she knew best.

Hello, firehouse.

"You've already seen the common room, obviously, which is really the main hub of the house," she said. "There are two wings on either side. One has the engine bay, the equipment room, and the captain's office"—she gestured down the hallway to the left—"and the other houses the bunks, the locker room, and a few small conference rooms. Any preference on where we go first?"

"Nope. You?" Finn asked back, pointing to the folder full of paperwork in her grasp. "I don't want to keep you from work. Not entirely, anyway."

January blinked. "Oh. Well, we have a pretty detailed filing system here, so I'm going to drop this off with Lieutenant Gamble. He's out on the call, obviously, but he and Lieutenant Hawkins on squad have small private bunks that double as offices."

"Great. That's this way then, right?"

Finn hooked a thumb to the right, starting to walk alongside her after she gave up a quick nod.

"So you're only in Remington for a few days," she said, and even though she'd tried to paint the words as small talk, keeping the curiosity out of her voice was damn near impossible.

"I've got a flight out early next week, yeah." Finn quickened his pace just enough to reach the glass double doors in their path before January did, tugging one open to usher her through. The move gave her a brief but magnificent view of his ass, and sweet Lord in heaven, hockey had been so. Very. Good to him.

"Right!" she exclaimed, wrestling her voice back down to normal-people levels before continuing with, "So this is a relatively quick trip, then."

Finn nodded, his boots thumping alongside her shiny black heels as he fell back into step beside her. "I only get the Cup for twenty-four hours; plus, I don't really know anyone around here anymore."

January's curiosity sparked back to life. "Not to be nosy, but why did you bring it to Remington then? Surely you've got a bajillion fans in New Orleans who would want a photo op with you and the Cup, not to mention a pack of teammates to celebrate with. What made you come all the way back here?"

"Asher's here."

Her heart went from zero to rapid-fire in two seconds flat. "You brought the Cup to Asher's grave?"

"This morning," Finn admitted. He slowed to a stop in the middle of the empty hallway, leaving January no choice but to do the same. "Look, I know you probably think I don't care about Asher, or that maybe I've forgotten him, but I haven't. In fact, he's the reason I ended up on the Rage. Without him, I never would've made that team, let alone won the Cup."

The shock in January's chest quickly slid into confusion. "I'm sorry. I don't follow."

"It's no secret I acted like an ass the night before I left town," Finn said, blowing out a breath and rocking back on the heels of his thickly soled boots. "But I was young and mad and stupid, and after the dust settled, I didn't know how to tell either one of you I knew I'd been a dick. Especially since you'd both been such good friends to me all through high school. My *only* friends."

"We were all young and stupid that night." January paused to fiddle with the edge of the folder still tucked in against the crook of her elbow, but Finn didn't budge as he looked her right in the eye.

"We might have all done things we regret that night, but I was the only one who was wrong. At the time, it was easier to pretend I didn't care than to admit I'd screwed up. Then enough time passed that I could pretend I didn't give a shit. But then..."

Realization trickled into her brain, and oh. *Oh God.* "Asher died."

"Asher died," Finn said, low and soft. "I had a thousand chances not to be an asshole. A million of them, maybe. But I was too dumb, too arrogant to know I wouldn't always have the chance."

"Finn." Emotion flickered through his whiskey-colored eyes, stealing her breath even farther. "No one could've known Asher was going to die in that house fire. He was doing his job. A job he loved."

"Yeah, but I shouldn't have waited to apologize. I

shouldn't have treated either of you the way that I did. Asher always believed in me. Not in an after-school special kind of way," he added, and here, she had to let go of a tiny smile.

"No. You'd have never let him get away with that."

Finn's exhale in reply fell just short of a puff of laughter. "You're right, I wouldn't. Asher always seemed to make the encouragement feel like the truth, though. And when he said I'd win the Cup one day, I believed him. I busted my ass to make him right, so he wouldn't think he'd put his faith in a fuck-up." Finn swallowed, shifting his weight over the linoleum. "When he died, I knew I had to do whatever it took to win the Cup. Not for me, but to be the person he thought I was before I let everything go to shit. So that's why I came back to Remington with it. To finally give him the apology he deserved."

January looked at him, the pang in her rib cage at odds with the thread of divisiveness she was unable to keep out of her tone as she said, "Asher wasn't the only person who believed in you, Finn."

"I know." He stepped toward her until only a few feet of space separated them in the brightly lit hallway. "I wanted to say something to you at the funeral, but I was so blindsided by Asher's death, none of it felt real. I knew you had your old man and everyone here at Seventeen to lean on, and I'd already hurt you."

Finn's voice turned to gravel over his last two words, and as hard as she knew this had to be for him, she wasn't about to sprinkle the truth with sugar just so she could call it candy, either. "You did hurt me."

"I guess I was grieving in my own screwed up way, and I didn't want to make things worse. It's not an excuse, but it is the truth. I'm really sorry I hurt you."

"Oh," January breathed, more sound than actual word. But his apology was so gruffly genuine, just like the Finn she

"The Rage isn't the only team in the league, Donnelly."

Finn lowered the empty coffee cup he'd pulled from an overhead cabinet, the china meeting the marble with a hard clink. "You've had offers from other teams?"

"I've had interest from other teams," Marty corrected, and Finn cut right to the chase.

"Are they talking about enough money to make this conversation worth my while?"

The silence on the other end of the line inspired zero confidence. "Donnelly, listen. It's not always about what these teams are willing to pay upfront—"

In an instant, Finn lost the fight with his frustration. "No. I don't give a shit about the maybes and the let's-sees. The Rage is my team, and I've more than earned my keep there. I'm not leaving New Orleans."

Marty stayed true to form—not that Finn had expected anything less. "I know you want the recognition you deserve, and I get that you're tight with those guys in Nola. I do. All I'm saying is, you're twenty-five. Your entire future is in front of you, and the Rage isn't jumping in with an offer right out of the gate. Maybe you should consider every option."

Finn opened his mouth, but closed it just shy of his response. There was no way he could explain to Marty— Christ, to *anyone*—that the only place he'd ever belonged was on that team. He might not have a family, or friends outside of his teammates, or a home that didn't involve pads and pucks and a shitload of ice. But Finn had hockey. He had the Rage.

He'd earned his spot there with three years' worth of blood, sweat, and tears, and he was going to goddamn well keep it at fair market value.

"I understand there might be interest from other teams," Finn said quietly. "But *I'm* only interested in getting the offer we all know I worked my ass off for, and the only team I'm interested in getting it from is the Rage."

Marty exhaled but thankfully didn't argue. "Well then. I guess I'd better keep that lunch meeting today with Babineaux. There's nothing quite like reminding a team owner how spectacular one of his players is when the guy is up for a new contract."

Finn let his hard-edged smile creep into his voice. "Come on, Marty. We both know you don't hate playing hardball." The guy's shrewd, no-bullshit nature was half the reason Finn had hired him in the first place.

"Eh, you may be right," Marty said, backing up the no-bullshit thing in spades. "I'll work on the suits and keep you posted. In the meantime, your day with the Cup is half over. Do me a favor and at least try to take a picture with the thing? The more good PR Babineaux sees, the happier the son of a bitch gets."

"I'll see what I can do," Finn said.

But as soon as the words left his mouth, he knew they were a lie.

~

FINN WAITED until he was on the threshold of January's condo to realize he probably should've brought her flowers. Then again, as much as he wanted to atone for having been a complete prick in the past, if he *had* brought her flowers, she might think this was a date. Not that taking her on a date would be a bad thing, necessarily, but he'd just freed up the top spot on her shit list after a seven year run. The least he could do was have the decency *not* to let his dick take point on their night out.

Unless she wanted him to, in which case...

"Oh for Chrissake," Finn muttered, placing a trio of

knocks on the door in front of him. This was January he was talking about. January, who had seen him sweaty and surly and sometimes even bloody after Tier 1 junior league games. January, who used to make him tell her when it was safe to look again during horror movies.

January, who had just opened the door to greet him, and *fuck*, he should've brought her flowers.

"Whoa," Finn said, taking a step back into the hallway. "You look…"

Although several words came to mind, none of them seemed quite powerful enough to do her justice. Her blond hair had been tucked into a low twist behind one ear, with a few wisps escaping to frame her face. A pair of shimmery silver earrings hung in thin threads that nearly brushed her shoulders, but it was her dress that had Finn biting back a groan. Last night, he'd been certain January's jeans were going to be the death of him. But they were nothing compared to the column of slate gray material clinging to her curves and hanging from the slender line of her shoulders by nothing more than the thinnest of shiny silver straps, and Jesus Christ, didn't this woman own a single scrap of clothing that wouldn't give him a raging hard-on in public?

"Thanks." Flushing slightly, January gave up a ta-da style twirl that did nothing to restore Finn's composure. "You look really nice too."

He laughed. "I got lucky. Suit shopping on the fly isn't for the faint of heart." Thankfully, both the salesman and the in-house tailor had been hockey fans and had been willing to hook him up.

"Ah. Well I'm exhausting my only fashion option for this evening." January gestured to the hallway in an unspoken *shall we?* and Finn nodded, offering his elbow.

"Something tells me you don't wear this to the firehouse."

"Yes and no, actually," she said, grabbing his attention.

"This is my go-to dress for the RFD's annual fundraiser. It's usually a big deal gala-type event."

"That sounds nice," he ventured warily, but her laugh in response told him he'd been flat-out busted.

"Sure. If you like staid and stuffy, it's fantastic."

Finn reached out to open the door for her, leading her to the rented SUV he'd parked in front of her building. "A fancy party doesn't seem like the best fit for a bunch of firefighters," he admitted.

"In truth, it's not. But the people with the deepest pockets tend to be Remington's Who's Who, and they like to be wowed. That's why we've always done a gala in the past, but I'll admit, with the steady decline in attendance and donations we've seen at recent events, I think this year is going to be a challenge."

"You sound like you have a pretty vested interest," Finn said, and January waited until he'd ushered her into the passenger seat, then gotten in to start the SUV before lifting her hands in pure *you got me* style.

"I volunteered to chair the event this year."

"Damn." He'd been to enough charity fundraisers for the Rage to know that planning one was a massive undertaking, even on a good day. But organizing an event like that as a volunteer? "That's pretty impressive."

January's tart laughter made Finn consider repeating himself, just so she'd keep it up. "I don't know if it's so much impressive rather than slightly crazy. The fundraiser is in a month, and the previous chairperson just skipped town to move in with her boyfriend in Chicago. Of course, that was after she did basically nothing by way of legwork, so I inherited a bit of an uphill climb."

"Okay, you win. That does sound slightly crazy."

"I know," she said. "But if we hit our fundraising goal, five firehouses in the district—including Station Seventeen

—will get new, state-of-the-art masks. The thermal imaging built into the equipment offers a substantial increase in visibility, which obviously helps the firefighters see potential hazards and find people more easily in burning buildings. Not to mention keeping them a whole lot safer on fire calls because they can get in and out faster."

Finn followed the directions on the GPS, his thoughts tumbling. "There have been a ton of advances in sports gear, helmets in particular. It's pretty cool to know that sort of technology exists for first responders too."

"That technology comes at a cost, though," January said, her frown audible.

"How much are we talking?"

"Over six hundred dollars a pop, and that's not even counting the compatible lighter-weight SCBA tanks, which can be just as expensive."

Holy... "Damn. No wonder the equipment isn't in the city's budget," Finn managed, and January gave up a resigned nod.

"Especially since between engine and squad, there are eight firefighters at Station Seventeen alone. But if we can get the gear in even one firehouse, it'll be worth the effort." Her smile grew again, brightening her face in the waning evening sunlight. "So I don't really mind putting in the extra hours to plan the fundraiser."

Finn took her in with a sidelong glance. "You really keep that place afloat, don't you? Making schedules and keeping everything running smoothly so those guys can do their jobs without thinking twice."

Being a woman of her word, January had taken him on a complete tour of the firehouse while he'd waited for the firefighters and paramedics to return from their call, showing him everything from the engine bay to the equipment room.

It had been all too easy to see how organized everything was, and how hard January had worked to get it that way.

Not that she seemed to think she'd gone above and beyond. "Sure," she said, one shoulder lifting in a demi-shrug. "I guess I have a pretty good handle on the day-to-day operations at Seventeen."

"*Pretty* good? You created a filing system that was implemented in every firehouse in the city last year, not to mention at RFD headquarters." Finn rode out the shock on her face for a second before caving in to add, "Your captain likes to brag about you. He told me about it after they got back from their call."

"Okay, first of all, I only came up with a new filing system because the old one was stupid, and everyone else just happened to like the way mine works," January argued, albeit without heat. "Secondly, I might work hard to make the administrative side of the firehouse run smoothly, but that's what the department hired me to do."

Finn swallowed the urge to laugh even though damn, it was strong. "You seem to go pretty far above and beyond normal job requirements, January—and before you argue and tell me 'it's nothing', remember I'm a workaholic too. I know one when I see one."

Laughing softly, she said, "Okay, maybe a little, but come on. I love my job, and those guys are like family. Plus, they risk an awful lot."

"They do," Finn agreed, his stomach knotting at the all-too-stark reality of exactly how much was on the line during fire calls. "They're still lucky to have you looking out for them."

"Thank you." January's cheeks colored a far too sexy shade of pink. Luckily for Finn's libido, they arrived at the restaurant before he could dwell on all the parts of her that might flush the same color under the right circumstances, and he handed the SUV over to the valet. Turning to escort her up the spotless dark red runner leading to a set of heavy double doors, they'd barely made it four steps over the Italian marble floors before the restaurant manager greeted them with a smile.

"Mr. Donnelly, how lovely to see you and your guest. Chef Rossi is thrilled to be preparing her signature tasting menu for you both this evening. Your table upstairs in the Skyline Room is ready and waiting. Right this way, please."

"Okay," January murmured once they'd been seated in a plush semi-circular booth with an admittedly spectacular view of the city. "So really, how did you manage this? Because I'm fairly certain we're sitting at the best table in the house, and a personal tasting menu from Angelina Rossi on a Friday night is practically unheard of."

He lifted one suit-clad shoulder, then casually let it drop. "I just came in earlier today and asked to speak with the manager. He was very accommodating."

"Oh, is that all?" Her expression broadcast her doubt loud and freaking clear, and ah hell, of course she was too smart for that. He might as well come clean.

"That, and I brought the Cup with me." Finn might not have wanted to make a big deal (okay, *any* deal) about having the Cup for the day, but he had to admit, seeing everyone's excitement over the thing at both the firehouse and the restaurant had been pretty cool. The chef had even been impressed enough to offer the tasting menu.

January laughed. "Between that and your charm, I really shouldn't be surprised."

One honey-colored eyebrow arched, and even though Finn knew he shouldn't flirt with her, the sassy little look on her face turned him on too much to resist.

"I told you to pick whatever you wanted," he said, letting the insinuation hang in the slight, softly lit space between them. "Now are you going to let me give it to you, or not?"

But she didn't even blink as she leaned in toward him, and fuck if that didn't turn Finn on even more. "So that's the deal? Tonight, I get whatever I want?"

His cock tightened along with his voice. "That's the deal."

"Good. Because you and I have a lot of catching up to do, and I don't plan on wasting a second."

CHAPTER 5

January was having an out of body experience. But between the rich decadence of the pinot noir the waiter had brought out to accompany their tasting menu and the borderline extravagant atmosphere of the cozy, candlelit dining room, everything around her was surreal.

And that was before she factored in the drop-dead gorgeous man sitting less than two feet away from her.

Covertly, she slid a glance at Finn as he listened to the waiter describe the different whiskeys available from La Lumière's private reserve. Although January had spent over an hour with him this morning at Station Seventeen (not to mention nearly five years as his best friend), the difference between gruff, tough, T-shirt-and-jeans-Finn and the Finn beside her put night and day to shame. He'd shaved and (mostly) tamed his dark hair, which curled softly over his ears and at the nape of his neck. His black suit was cut to perfection, flawlessly outlining his broad shoulders as his charcoal-colored shirt did the same for the lean, muscular plane of his chest, and oh God, there was no way around the truth.

He might only be here for a few days, but she wanted Finn Donnelly.

Bad.

"So," January said with a shade more enthusiasm than necessary. "This view is honestly incredible. Although being a famous hockey player, you've probably seen your fair share of swanky restaurants."

"The view is stunning," Finn replied, keeping his gaze firmly fastened to hers as he spoke, and January's heart thrummed faster in her chest. "But I'm hardly fancy. Or famous."

Her laughter popped out, scattering her nerves along the way. "Uh, you play a highly popular sport at the professional level. The anchors on *SportsCenter* nicknamed you and Flynn Kazakov 'The F-Bombs', for Pete's sake. I hate to be the bearer of bad news, but you aren't exactly small potatoes."

"Okay, how about this? I don't *feel* famous. Although I will admit, the thing with Kazakov is pretty accurate." Finn paused as the waiter quietly delivered his drink, the amber liquid glinting against the intricately cut crystal as Finn lifted it for a sip before continuing. "I mean, I travel a lot, which is pretty cool, and sometimes I get recognized if I'm out in New Orleans, but other than that, I'm still just a guy who likes to play hockey."

"Funny, I'm still just a girl who likes to watch hockey," January said, and Finn assessed her with a smirk that made the space between her hips flood with heat.

"You still a Rogues fan?"

Of course he would remember how diehard she was for the Charlotte-based team. "Maybe."

"A yes if I ever heard one. For the record, your poker face still sucks."

January caved, but only because she had no other choice.

"I'm a hometown girl, born and bred. So sue me. Do you like New Orleans?"

"I'm obviously on the road a lot, but yeah. It's home."

His smile was completely at odds with the noncommittal tone he'd tried to pin to the words, and it looked like her poker face wasn't the only one that needed some polishing.

"A yes if I ever heard one," she volleyed, running a finger around the rim of her wine glass. "You seem to have some nice camaraderie with the guys on the Rage."

"You follow the Rage?" His brows betrayed his surprise by traveling up toward his tousled hairline, but January met his flirty look with one of her own.

"Just because I was mad at you doesn't mean I'm blind, Finnegan. The Rage's Cinderella season was pretty tough to miss."

She saw the intention of a smart reply flicker through his eyes in the soft light of the restaurant, and her belly tightened in anticipation. But he pulled it back just shy of launch, opting for another draw from his glass before going with, "Yeah, the guys and I are tight. I'm up for a new contract right now, and when I get it, New Orleans will be home for a good long time. It's actually the other reason I came back here."

Now *that* got her attention. "Oh?"

Finn lifted his chin in a barely there nod, his expression suddenly serious. "When my old man died, he left me his house."

"The one over in North Point?"

He'd never been particularly chatty about his family, but the fact that his father had never attended a single one of his hockey games—not even the Tier 1 championship game where Finn had scored a hat trick that included the game-winning goal at the buzzer—had spoken volumes. Along with the fact that in nearly five years of best friendship with

Finn, January had never met the man, nor had she ever been to the house in question.

"Yeah." Finn's shoulders tightened against the high back of the booth, forming a rigid line beneath the crisp fabric of his suit jacket. "He never moved after I left. Lived there until…you know."

For a second, January considered an about-face subject change. But she'd never shied away from anything with Finn in the past. Starting now seemed stupid.

"I was sorry to hear that he'd passed away," she said, reaching out to brush her fingers over his. Although the obituary had oddly not mentioned Finn, or anyone at all in terms of family, there weren't too many Seamus Donnellys in Remington. She'd connected the dots with ease when she'd read it in the paper the year before last.

"Don't be." Seeming to hear the rough edges of his words after they'd emerged, Finn added, "I mean, that's really nice of you. But he'd been sick for a long time, and we weren't tight. Anyway." He threw back the rest of the liquor in his glass in one quick movement. "I figured since I'd be here in Remington and I've got a little time now that it's the off-season, I'd go ahead and meet with a realtor to get the place on the market."

"Wow." January's heart kicked beneath the thin silk of her dress. "You really are tying up loose ends, huh?"

Finn nodded. "Guess it's just time," he said, his expression softening by a degree before he continued. "What about you? Are you and your old man still thick as thieves?"

January's smile was as quick as it was genuine as she thought of her own father. "Of course. He's running the intelligence unit at the Thirty-Third now. They catch all sorts of crazy cases. Last fall they broke up a huge forced prostitution ring. A couple of national news outlets even picked up the story."

"Damn." The look on Finn's face was both reverent and impressed. "He's running the whole unit? Guess you come by that workaholic side of yours honestly."

"My father raised me all by himself, and I've always been a quintessential Daddy's Girl," she reminded him with a laugh. "Did you really think I wouldn't follow in his footsteps as far as my work habits are concerned?"

"Truth? Not even for a second," Finn said with a laugh of his own.

The conversation shifted back to work and family (her) and hockey (him). With each passing course in the tasting menu, the laughter—and the wine—flowed a little more freely. For every story January told him about working at Station Seventeen, Finn matched it with one from the Rage, until finally, she was certain that Cup or no, the manager was going to come boot them from their table for having more fun than should be allowed in public.

"You seriously had a guy on squad put Kool-Aid powder in another firefighter's gloves?" Finn asked, his eyes all mischief.

January finished the last of her pinot noir before grinning in affirmation. "The firefighters don't usually mess with each other's gear too much for safety reasons, but yeah. Dempsey went all-in, too. Purple in one glove and blue in the other. Faurier sweat himself right into a rainbow."

"Please tell me it stains. Because I owe our right-winger Ford Callaghan one, and that would be priceless."

"For about three days," January confirmed. Tucking an errant strand of loose hair behind her ear, she sat back against the booth, a pang of nostalgia moving through her chest. Falling back into step with Finn had been so seamless, and God, she'd spent so much time being mad at him that she hadn't fully realized how much she'd *missed* him.

"This was really nice," she said, twirling her finger to

encircle the two of them in an invisible loop. "Seeing you again and being able to catch up."

"Nice?" Finn's lips curved with a hint of wickedness that made her blush a foregone conclusion. "I'm thinking I need to up my game."

"Believe me, your game doesn't need a thing."

She heard the words only after they were out, her cheeks flushing in their wake. God, hadn't she learned her lesson when she'd tried to kiss him seven years ago? Finn might have taken her to dinner to make up for shutting her out after he'd left Remington, and yeah, he'd borderline flirted with her tonight, just as he had all through high school. But he borderline flirted with nearly all women, and he'd been wildly clear the night she'd kissed him. He saw her as a friend. Nothing more.

Finn cleared his throat and shifted back, but mercifully glossed over her verbal indiscretion. "So what now?"

"Wasn't this enough?" Brows sky-high, January gestured to the mostly empty dessert plates and the definitely empty wine glasses on the table in front of them, but funny, he didn't budge.

"No."

"No?" She tried—truly—to keep her shock under wraps, but between Finn's unyielding expression and the absolute certainty of his answer, it was pretty much a total no-go.

"You said it yourself, right? Catching up has been *nice*." His tone laced around the word with just enough teasing humor to lighten the mood. "And I do have seven years to make up for."

"After tonight?" January sent a glance around the lush, candlelit restaurant and laughed. "I think we're even."

"Oh, I think we're just getting started. They still run the fountains in front of the Plaza on the weekends, right?"

"Yeah." She stretched her answer out into a question. The

fountains in front of the Plaza hotel were one of the biggest attractions in all of Remington. Rather than being set in a traditional pool, though, like the huge shows in Las Vegas, they were arranged over the flagstones in front of the hotel itself, so people could get as up close and personal with the aquatics display as they dared. The fountains had always been one of January's favorite things, even if she did manage to miscalculate the timing of the spray and get soaked way more often than not.

A fact which Finn clearly remembered. "What do you say we go tempt fate a little and check it out?"

Attraction pulled, low and deep in January's belly. Between the glint in his eye and the dare in his voice, Finn was tempting so much more than fate. But the truth was, she *had* missed him. What's more, she didn't want their night to end just yet, either.

"I say be careful what you wish for, Finnegan Donnelly. You just might get it."

A few quick actions had their check taken care of and Finn's SUV brought around by the valet, and a few quick minutes had them back at the Plaza. Although the sun had long since set, the night air was warm enough to still be plenty comfortable as they walked around to the front of the five-story hotel. She was a bit surprised they had the impending display to themselves, although it *was* getting late, and it looked as if the last show had been over for a while, the bystanders obviously scattered.

"I take it the waterworks are still timed," Finn said, pointing toward the wide circle of flagstones gleaming in the soft light being cast down from the Plaza behind them. A half-wall of stacked stone ringed the area in four arcs around the fountains, beyond which only the bravest (or the most waterproof) people ventured, and January's heels clicked to a stop just shy of the nearest one.

"Mmm hmm. There's a ten-minute show at the top of every hour on the weekend. They added colored lights to the mix a few years ago, too. The added effect on the water is really cool."

"Sounds like I've missed a thing or two since I've been gone."

Finn shifted, the sleeve of his jacket brushing over her bare skin enough to capture her breath in her throat. Unable to help it, January shivered, making Finn's brow tuck slightly in concern.

"Are you cold?" He moved to start sliding his jacket from his shoulders, but oh God, Finn in less clothes would probably send her right over the edge.

"Oh, no. I'm…" *Definitely not cold. Definitely still attracted to you. Definitely dying for you to lift up my dress and do dirty, unspeakable, orgasm-worthy things to me until I can't remember my name.* "Good! Good. I'm good." Also, a complete and utter tangle of horny-girl hormones, but now *so* wasn't the time to split hairs.

"Shitty poker face," Finn reminded her. "Here, take my jacket."

He was out of the thing before January could renew her protest. Slipping the material over her shoulders, he turned her to straighten the jacket into place. The move put them face to face, their bodies so close that she could feel the heat of his exhale as it coasted over her cheek, and her sex clenched with need. She'd wanted Finn so much for so long, and here he was, right in front of her after seven years.

Her heart slammed, but her mouth opened anyway. "Finn, I—"

Before she could say anything else, the fountains sprang to life. Finn didn't so much as flinch—which made one of them, at least— and he reached down to find her fingers beneath the too-long sleeve of her borrowed jacket instead.

"Did you still want to tempt fate?"

His stare flickered over the water arcing up in gentle waves, some high, some lower, all of them moving in tandem to an unspoken rhythm. January nodded, a smile taking over her mouth as she curled her hand around his. Finn returned his stare to hers, but only for a second before he shocked the hell out of her by turning toward the break in the wall and leading her closer to the water.

"Maybe you should be careful what *you* wish for. When I tempt fate, I go all in."

Without so much as another word, he stepped over the threshold of the outer circle of flagstones. The mist from the fountains settled over them in a cool spray, and January's lips parted in a gasp of surprise.

"This is crazy!" she said, although she was laughing hard enough to seriously weaken any heat her protest might have carried. "We're going to get soaked."

"We might," he agreed, his expression bordering on cocky as he tugged her even closer to the ever-changing streams of water pushing up from the softly lit pathway. "But look." With his free hand, Finn pointed to the row of fountains closest to them, where the water was barely bubbling a few feet high. "Most bathtubs aren't even that deep, and the water runs off to the drain set into flagstones. I bet we can get a little closer without getting drenched. Come on." Another pull, and they were so daringly close to the fountains that excitement prickled beneath January's skin.

"Oh, *look*. It's so pretty from here." This close, the water glittered and danced in the lights shining up from the pavers. Unable to resist the thrilling temptation, January swung around, this time leading Finn toward the next row of fountains. But just as they took the last step, the cadence of the water changed, all of the jets spraying at once.

"Oh my God!" The exclamation burst past a fresh peal of

laughter as a light rain fell all around them. Finn's laughter twined around hers, and after three steps of trying to navigate them back to safety, he gave up, turning to scoop her off her feet as he bolted back through the spray.

"Okay, okay," he said, setting her heels down and grinning broadly once they'd cleared the reach of the water. "You might've been right about us getting soaked."

In that moment, January became hyper-aware of how close they were, of every place where Finn's body came in contact with hers. His arms were still wrapped around her shoulders, droplets of water clinging to his dark, decadent eyelashes, his smiling mouth only inches from hers. Want rippled down her spine, pooling low and hot between her thighs, but she didn't fight it.

"I kissed you seven years ago," she whispered, her voice trembling despite her best efforts to keep it steady.

Finn slid a hand up to cup her face. "Do it again."

January exhaled, just a small sound of surprise. "But you said you didn't look at me that way. That night, you said—"

"I lied."

"You *lied*?" Her pulse stuttered, her brain spinning as she tried to process what he'd said, but he slid his opposite hand over her hip to pull their bodies flush.

"I fucking lied. I knew Asher had feelings for you, so I lied about mine. But I've wanted you since the minute I laid eyes on you, so please. Either kiss me or I'm kissing you. I'm happy to do the honors." Finn's eyes dropped to her mouth, glinting with intention before he lifted his gaze back to hers, pinning her into place. "But I'd be even happier if you'd take what you wanted all those years ago instead."

January pressed up to fit her lips to his in a rush. For a second, Finn just stood there, as if he was surprised she'd actually kissed him. Then his fingers drifted lower to press against the column of her neck, and she was lost. Arching up against him, her tongue swept out for a brash taste. Finn opened for her with ease, letting her take the lead, and January didn't think twice. Her arms flew over his shoulders as she anchored herself against his firm, full lips, testing and taking as she deepened the kiss. Somewhere, in the rational part of her brain that felt very far away, she realized that even though the lights were dim and the area had been deserted when they'd arrived, she and Finn were still outside in front of the hotel.

But oh God, she didn't care. With the way Finn was pushed up against her, hard and hot in the best possible places, all January could think was *more*.

His tongue slipped against hers, seeking and claiming all at once before he broke contact to trail his mouth in a slow path over the line of her jaw. "Be sure," he grated, closing his teeth over her earlobe with just enough pressure to make her clit throb with greedy need, and she hooked her arms around the ridge of his shoulders even tighter. Yes, this was crazy, but she'd always been crazy where Finn was concerned. Just like she was one hundred percent certain she wanted him right now.

"I'm sure. Now do that again."

He made a noise between a laugh and a growl before sending the edge of his teeth over her earlobe in a repeat pass. January's nipples hardened, aching to be touched and stroked and sucked, and Finn's hand drifted up from her hip to her rib cage as if he'd read her mind.

"You look so pretty like this, all flushed and ready. I almost want to find some dark corner so I can drop to my knees and make you come right now, just to find out if you sound as pretty as you look."

Her pulse slammed faster at the suggestion, and the edges of Finn's mouth kicked into a dark, sexy smile at the want-filled sigh that drifted past her lips.

"Would you like that?" he asked, redirecting the path of his hand from her torso back to her hip. January nearly whimpered in frustration, but the urge met a quick end when his stare grew even darker than his smile. "Do you want me to put my mouth on your sweet little pussy and taste you until you come undone?"

The bold, dirty words should've shocked her, she knew. But the way Finn said them, so full of promise and raw honesty, only made her want him to turn them into hard, fast action.

So she pushed up to kiss him, just one firm press of her mouth before she said, "Yes. Now take me upstairs to your room. I've spent seven years fucking you in my mind, and it's time to turn all these fantasies into reality."

CHAPTER 6

To anyone milling around the lobby of the Plaza, Finn and January probably looked like any other couple coming back from a night on the town. But as he politely offered her his arm and led her into the elegantly mirrored elevator that went up to the penthouse suite, it took every last ounce of restraint on the planet for him not to shove her dress up to her hips and fuck her until she screamed.

They rode upstairs in total silence. Although they were both more than a little damp from their run through the fountains, January still looked goddamned exquisite, her face flushed and her hair breaking free from the twist at her nape. Their shoulders barely touched as they stood side by side, but Christ, the sexual tension filled the air around them like an electric charge, making Finn's heart pound faster with each passing floor. Finally, they made their way from the elevator to the threshold of his suite, and after some quick work with the key card, he ushered January into the shadowy space.

"Thank you," she murmured, the same way she might thank him for a cup of coffee or for saying *God bless you* after she sneezed. But as soon as the door clicked shut, they turned simultaneously, crashing together in a tangle of tongues and limbs and intentions so bad, his cock grew rockhard in an instant.

"You're welcome," Finn said, his voice rough with want. "Now come here and let me make good on my promise."

Knotting a hand in her hair and wrapping his other arm around her waist, he pulled her against his body in one swift yank, barely stifling a moan as soon as their chests made contact. She was so soft, so full of lush, hot curves yet strong at the same time, that Finn wanted to take his time and taste her everywhere.

Starting with more of her mouth.

Pulling back just enough to gain leverage, he swiped his tongue over the seam of January's lips. They parted, the needful exhale that accompanied the movement sending a shot of lust deep through Finn's belly, and the hand in her hair tightened of its own accord. The tiny part of his mind that housed his decency warned him how firmly he'd gripped, how badly he *wanted*, and he made to loosen his fingers. But then January pressed up to kiss him just as hard, and Finn thrust against her with even more reckless desire.

"Do you have any idea what you're doing to me when you kiss me like that?" he asked. His lips still touched hers—because hell if he was willing to fully break the connection with her sweet, sinful mouth—and she surprised him with a throaty laugh.

"What? Like this?" January broke off to skate her tongue over his in a movement caught somewhere between teasing and taking. The coyness in her words was completely at odds with the sexiness in her voice as she said them, and both combined to make Finn's pulse rush in his ears. Keeping his hold on her hip and her shoulder, he moved forward until

over yet another plea to give her what she'd waited so long to have.

No more waiting.

Finn closed his lips over her clit, pulling the rigid knot into his mouth with a firm suck. The cry that tore from her throat made his heart pound and his cock stiff enough to border on pain, but still, he didn't stop. Working her with his tongue, Finn licked and sucked and circled until January's thighs began to tremble.

Yes. Yes. Fucking *yes*. "Take it," he urged, swiping his tongue back over her clit in a hard swirl. "Show me what you taste like when you come undone."

Her tremble grew into a full-on tightening, her body holding steady for just a breath before she came with a keening cry. Finn stilled, letting her take what she wanted, however she wanted it, before slowly scaling back on his touch and finding his feet.

"You're pretty incredible," he said, surprised as hell when January laughed, long and loud in reply.

"You just gave me the best orgasm I've ever freaking had, and *I'm* incredible?"

As much as Finn didn't want to lose the mood, there was pretty much no way he could let that go. "The best, huh?"

January's eyes glinted in the shadows. One barely-there shrug sent the suit jacket from her shoulders to the floor, a lightning fast turn of her wrist and hiss of her zipper had her dress following in its path.

"Mmm hmm," she confirmed, utterly confident despite her nakedness. "Is tonight still about whatever I want?"

His cock jerked. "Yes."

"Then take me to bed so I can return the favor."

Finn pulled her closer to slam his mouth over hers in answer. They moved across the suite in a flurry of deep kisses, hastily discarding most of his clothes along the way.

He led January to the threshold of his bedroom, lifting her off her feet and placing her in the center of the snowy white duvet. Strains of moonlight and city lights filtered in past the sheer curtains, and both combined to offer just enough visibility in the shadows. Finn took a brief but necessary minute to grab a condom from his bag in the adjacent bathroom, and January reached out to close the space between them as soon as he returned to the bed.

"Come here." She opened her knees in invitation, leaning back against the lush pillows. Propping as much of his weight as possible on one forearm, he lowered himself against her, bringing their bodies flush from mouths to chests to hips.

"Ah, God," Finn grated, thrusting his cock into the cradle of her hips even though his boxer briefs were still firmly in place.

January thrust back, the seam of her body hot and wet through the fabric. "Don't make me wait, Finn. I want you inside me. I want to know what *you* sound like when you come."

She reached between them, her fingers curling around the gray cotton at his waist, and Finn was done holding back. His boxer briefs were off in an instant, the condom safely in place in another, and before he could think or breathe or control a single goddamn thing about his actions, he filled January's pussy in one unforgiving stroke.

Oh. Holy. Hell.

For a second, Finn was paralyzed by all the uncut sensations taking over his body and brain. Although he'd slid into her with ease, January's inner muscles squeezed tightly around his cock, sending his breath to a near-halt in his lungs. She dug her fingers into his shoulders, the sweet sting of her nails turning to all pleasure as her back arched against the covers, her nipples pebbled with obvious arousal. The sound coming up from Finn's throat meant to be a moan, but then January moved—just a tiny retreat of her hips was all it took—and his chest vibrated with a growl.

"January." His hands turned to hot fists, gripping the bedsheets as he levered back. The next press forward brought even more hot pressure around his shaft, and Finn couldn't tell what he wanted more—to fuck her harder or fuck her longer. But then she reached around his waist, spreading her fingers wide on either side of his ass to keep his cock locked inside of her, and the decision became involuntary. Digging his knees into the mattress, he rocked against her body over and over until they'd built a hard, fast cadence between them. Every thrust brought him closer—more intensity, more slick heat, more *everything*—and January looked up at him with a glittering stare.

"You don't have to hold back. Take it, Finn. Take what you want."

The words landed deep in his chest, shredding the last of his control. He pistoned his hips, his cock filling her to the hilt with each thrust, and she shuddered in response, calling Finn's name. His climax came on fast and strong, rising from the base of his spine to his balls, and he buried himself inside her as he came with a shout.

Minutes passed, his body going lax and his breathing slowing from ragged gasps to a somewhat smoother rhythm. Finn shifted to January's side so he didn't crush her, giving himself an extra minute to make sure his legs would actually do the job of supporting his body weight before taking a quick trip to the bathroom to clean up. When he returned, January was still on the bed, but she'd pulled the covers over her, tucking them over her chest and beneath both arms.

"Hey," she said, and even though the word was only a whisper, Finn would've heard the hitch from a thousand yards away.

"What's the matter?"

She laughed, but it was more irony than humor. "Nothing. I just, ah. Didn't expect we'd end up here tonight."

"I didn't either," Finn admitted. "I'm glad we did, though."

That seemed to surprise her. "You are?"

Surprise moved through Finn right back. "Aren't you?"

"Of course," she said, her answer immediate. "It's just...we don't have to make this awkward by turning it into something it's not just because we were close once. I know you're only in Remington for a few days."

Finn blew a breath into the shadows. This was the point at which he usually agreed wholeheartedly, telling whoever happened to be in his bed that yeah, he was going to be on a plane/train/bus/whatever in the very near future. But even though that was true in this case too, something made him say, "Okay, but that doesn't mean we can't spend those few days together."

"You want me to stay?" January asked, blinking at him through the velvety ambient light in the bedroom.

Finn's heart kicked against his sternum. He might have hidden his feelings from her in the past, but he had never, ever lied to her outright. No matter how fleeting this might be, he wasn't about to start now. "Sure. This is still your night. Come on, what do you want to do now? Name it, and I'll make it happen."

She answered after a pause. "You're going to laugh."

"I will not." He crossed a finger over his chest as proof.

"Even if I tell you I want to watch horror movies on Pay-Per-View and make you tell me when I can look again after all the really scary parts?"

Shit. "Okay, I might be laughing at you a little. But if a movie marathon is what you want..." He reached for the remote, pulling her close. "I'm game, Calendar Girl."

Just for tonight, it was enough.

CHAPTER 7

J anuary woke slowly, burrowing deeper in the hypnotic warmth of the butter-soft bedsheets. Her mind drifted over the last twelve hours, lazily reminding her of dinner...the impulsive trip to the fountains in front of the hotel...Finn's rough, gruff voice as he'd told her to come...the intensity on his gorgeous face when she'd said it right back to him...the night they'd spent together after that, wrapped up in blankets and laughter and each other as they'd watched movies until drifting off...

Oh God, she'd had insanely hot, other-worldly, mind-blowing sex with Finn. *Finn*. And rather than rationally thinking about the fact that he was going back to New Orleans in a few days, probably forever, all January wanted was to do it again.

"Mmmm. Morning," Finn murmured, and okay, that sexy, scruffy, bed-head thing he had going on *so* wasn't helping to keep her libido in check.

"It is morning." Rolling over, she squinted at the clock on the bedside table, exhaling in surprise as the numbers registered. "Oh, it's early."

"I'm not much of a late sleeper," Finn admitted. "Occupational hazard."

January's brows rose. "What time does the team usually practice?"

"It depends on where we are in the season, but no matter when we hit the ice, I go in a couple hours early, just to do my own workout and review film."

The muscles in his shoulders flexed enticingly as he stretched, and January forced herself to focus. "Jeez. You really *are* a workaholic."

Finn turned to his side, facing her in the soft, early morning sunlight drifting in past the sheers. "Maybe. But playing hockey is all I've ever wanted to do. It doesn't feel like work to me."

"You haven't spent much time with the Cup," she said, her stomach giving up a tiny squeeze as his expression tightened in response.

"I only wanted to do one thing with it, and that was bring it to Asher's grave."

An idea sparked in January's mind, pushing past her lips before she could cage it. "You have it for another hour or so, right? Why don't we have breakfast with it?"

The edges of Finn's mouth lifted in a half-smirk. "You do realize Edwin comes with the deal?"

"Yes, I realize Edwin comes with the deal, but come on. It's the *Cup*, Finn. I know you wanted to bring it to Asher's grave rather than get all flashy with the thing, but you worked your ass off to earn the win. Don't you think you deserve a little celebration too?"

The surprise whisking through his light brown stare told her all too clearly that the thought hadn't occurred to him. "I guess I do have some time before Edwin takes the Cup to my buddy, Bear. But we'll need to hurry. Bear racked up more penalty minutes than anyone else on the Rage this year. He and I might be teammates, but I'm not about to piss the guy off by keeping him from his day with the Cup."

January pictured the big, burly defenseman in her head, and oookay. Valid point. "Alright. I'll jump in the shower while you order room service and talk to Edwin. Sound good?"

"You in the shower?" Just like that, Finn's stare grew hot. "That sounds *very* good."

Warmth pooled between her thighs, reminding her that they were very, very naked beneath the sheets. "Focus, Finnegan," she managed to say, sending an identical message to the part of her brain that wanted to chuck breakfast and have Finn instead. "You. Me. The Cup. Fifteen minutes."

"Okay, okay," he said, getting out of bed and reaching for the pair of jeans sitting on top of his duffel bag, bedside. "Fifteen minutes."

January slid from the covers and padded to the bathroom —which was the size of her entire condo and *way* fancier— letting the hot water run for a minute before stepping into the spray. There were plenty of hotel toiletries for her to go through her lather, rinse, repeat routine, which she did with efficiency even though a tiny part of her was tempted to linger beneath the multiple showerheads. She was halfway through drying off when she realized that her only clothing options were the towel currently wrapped around her and the dress she'd unceremoniously left in a puddle on the floor last night, and crap. Guess she'd have to wear one to go get the other. But as soon as she poked her head into the bedroom, she broke into a grin and scooped up option number three from where Finn had left it at the foot of the bed.

"Are you trying to sway my team loyalty?" she asked a minute later, giving a little twirl over the carpet of the suite's main room to show off the Rage jersey bearing Finn's number and the pair of sweatpants she'd had to roll a few times at the waist in order to keep from tripping or losing them outright.

Finn laughed, and *God* it sounded good. "Absolutely."

"Hmm." January crossed the room, pressing up to kiss him. "It might be working."

"Ahem."

The sound of a masculine throat that clearly wasn't Finn's being cleared made her pulse jump. "Oh!"

"You remember Edwin," Finn said with an I-told-you-so grin, and she had to laugh.

"Of course." She peeked over Finn's T-shirted shoulder at the Cup's keeper, who was seated in a leather chair on the far side of the suite. "Good morning, Edwin."

"Good morning, Ms. Sinclair."

"Would you like some coffee?" January asked, pulling back from Finn and pointing to the full pot sitting on the counter in the kitchenette (which was also way fancier than hers, thank you very much.)

Both Finn and Edwin fixed her with twin looks of shock, but Edwin found his voice first. "It isn't necessary for me to join you while you eat. My duties as the keeper only require me to be able to see the Cup." He sent a pointed glance to the item in question, which stood proudly on the desk situated halfway across the sweeping space of the suite. "I don't want to intrude."

"You're not intruding if you're invited," she said. As spacious as their surroundings were, they still had to all be in the same room in order to follow the rules. Even if she and Finn whispered, chances were high that Edwin would over-hear whatever they decided to talk about. Including the poor guy just seemed less awkward, not to mention more polite.

A fact that Finn seemed to agree with. "Sure, man. It's just breakfast."

"Oh." Edwin blinked from behind the thick frames of his glasses. "Well, I suppose I could join you then. As long as you're certain."

A couple of minutes had them situated around the dining table beside the kitchenette, with Finn pulling the domed covers off the half-dozen serving plates their room service waiter had delivered. January's gaze slid to the nearby desk, her belly doing a tiny flip at being this close to one of the most iconic sports trophies in the world.

"The Cup is beautiful," she said, taking in the details with a longer stare. "And also kind of gigantic."

"The Cup's dimensions do often surprise people when they see it in person," Edwin agreed. His eyes lit with excitement from behind his glasses, and he straightened his bowtie as he continued. "But it has to be sturdy enough to withstand not just going from winning team to winning team every year, but to be passed from player to player within any victorious season."

He launched into a rather fascinating history of the Cup that lasted for most of their breakfast. Although Finn stayed mostly quiet, alternating between drinking coffee and eating more bacon and eggs and home fries than was in any way fair for a man with abs like his, January caught him looking at the Cup enough times during the meal to know her suggestion had been a good one. She got a particular thrill when both Finn and Edwin encouraged her to hold the Cup, and was equally happy to clear the dishes so Finn could have some space with the trophy before Edwin packed it into its trunk and said his goodbyes.

"That was pretty amazing," January admitted, walking over to the spot where Finn was standing by the windows.

"It was cool of you to include Edwin, although after all those hockey stats you two just traded, I think he's a little bit in love with you." Finn reached out to pull her in close before adding, "Hopefully he's not impressed by your love for the Rogues."

"Do not mock my team." January tried for a stern frown, but her sigh at the feel of Finn's muscular arms around her pretty much canceled it out.

He arched a shadowy brow, melting her further with a slow, soft kiss. "Say whatever you want, Calendar Girl. I know whose jersey you're wearing."

She laughed, clearly busted. "I probably should go home and get dressed in clothes that actually belong to me."

"I don't know," Finn said, pulling back just enough to fix her with a sexy up-and-down appraisal. "You look pretty cute in my jersey."

"Maybe, but I'm not sure I look entirely appropriate for the recon I have to do today on the venue for this fundraiser."

His brows lifted, eyes going wider in the morning sunlight spilling in past the giant windows at his back. "The previous volunteer booked a venue before she took off. That's good, right?"

Oh, if only. "It would be if she hadn't chosen Chase Manor."

"Isn't that place like a hundred years old, and not in the good way?"

January's heart corkscrewed behind her sternum as she rolled her eyes and grumbled, "Don't remind me."

God, this fundraiser had disaster written all over it in bright red spray paint. Which her expression must have betrayed, because Finn said, "Tell you what. I've got an appointment with a realtor to go through my dad's place at two. If you want, we can be each other's moral support. I'll go with you to check out Chase Manor if you'll come with me to get the house on the market. How does that sound?"

"You want to go with me to help organize this fundraiser?" She stepped back on the carpet, surprise and something else she couldn't quite identify rippling through her.

"Do you really want to go alone?" he asked back, and her answer popped out, automatic.

"No."

"Okay, then. Let's get you back to your place so you can change." He jutted his chin at the door, a smirk kicking up amidst the hint of dark stubble on his jaw. "But go ahead and hang on to the jersey. I'm determined to make a Rage fan out of you yet."

～

FINN STOOD on the rickety front porch, looking up at the even more rickety house where he'd spent his adolescence. Dread put a bitter taste in his mouth despite the bright June sunshine and the gentle hint of a breeze taking just enough edge off the afternoon heat to keep the weather pleasant.

This trip to North Point? Not so fucking much.

"Hey." January reached out, brushing the side of her hand against his with a gentle bump that offered just enough support over pity. "You want to wait for the realtor before we go inside?"

"Yeah. She should be here any minute." Plus, it wasn't as if Finn would be getting all nostalgic once they crossed the (ramshackle) threshold. The quicker they could get this walk-through over with, the happier he'd be.

January's voice stayed light as she asked, "Are you okay?"

Finn lifted a shoulder, but only halfway. "The house is just in worse shape than I remember, I guess." He let his eyes flicker over the rotting porch boards, the badly peeling paint on the clapboard siding, and—shit—the section of chain link fence by the side yard that had all but caved in. "I'm a little scared about what the inside looks like."

"Hmm," she said, her pretty blue gaze following his. "Well, I guess we can look at the bright side."

"Which is?"

January waggled her brows, and funny, the movement put a huge dent in the tension in Finn's chest. "No matter what we find in there, it can't be as bad as Chase Manor."

As much as he hated to admit it... "You might be right there. That place was pretty bad."

"Look at you with the niceties." She laughed. "Chase Manor might've been upscale in its heyday, but that was forty years ago. The place is trapped in a bad seventies time warp, not to mention almost certainly violating both the fire code *and* the health code about a dozen different ways. I'm ninety percent sure the only reason Michelle booked it was because nothing else was available. Which sadly means I'm stuck with it, health code violations and all."

"You're pretty upbeat considering the circumstances."

January paced over the porch boards, her sandals thumping softly on the uneven, splintery planks. "Getting upset will only waste valuable energy. I'm not going to find a perfect, affordable, available new venue with a month to go. I've got to do the best I can with what I've got."

The slam of a car door sounded off from the street in front of them, cutting off Finn's response and tightening the air in his lungs. A woman in a navy blue suit approached the house, her assessing stare and the slight but definite frown that accompanied it doing exactly zip for his confidence.

"Mr. Donnelly? I'm Dana Levine, with Levine Realty. It's a pleasure to meet you."

"Finn, please." He shook her hand, introducing January before giving up a mental *screw it* and diving past the pleasantries. "The house isn't in the best condition, I know. Not that it was ever Shangri-La or anything."

Dana didn't argue, but at least she was nice enough not to

agree outright, either. "That's okay. Previously owned homes are almost never pristine. Why don't you show me around and we'll go from there?"

A tour of the house's two musty, dusty levels and highly dilapidated backyard didn't help either Finn's cause or Dana's frown.

"I had the place cleared out after my old man died. Obviously," he said, gesturing to the bare but dinged-up walls and matching carpets on the main level as the three of them came to a stop in the living room. "And I pay someone to come cut the grass in the summer. I guess I didn't realize an empty house would need more upkeep than that."

"Often, it doesn't," Dana said kindly. "But the house has been vacant for two years, and when the amenities haven't been updated for some time prior to a house sitting empty, it tends to make even the best maintenance difficult."

Finn looked around the room, taking in the awful light green walls and stained, faded carpet that his father had never made an effort to keep clean, let alone update. "I can still put it on the market though, right?"

"You can," Dana said slowly, shocking the crap out of him, and—if her brows-up, lips-parted expression was anything to go by—January too. "But as your potential realtor, I feel the need to be upfront with you. In this case, putting the house on the market and actually selling it are likely to be entirely different matters."

"So Finn would have to have some things replaced or repaired before the house would sell?" January asked, and Dana confirmed with a crisp nod.

"There are a lot of houses in this neighborhood that are already on the market in way better shape. Despite my best efforts, I don't think I could sell this one as-is."

Frustration welled in Finn's chest, and he damn near gave in to it. But then January brushed her hand against his, just like she had on the porch, and he managed to ask, "How much work are we talking about?"

"At bare minimum, I think you're looking at a good three weeks' worth of work to have the house painted inside and out, replace these carpets, and have repairs done to the roof, the porch, and the back deck. I know that's likely not what you wanted to hear." Dana gestured to the dingy space around them, and dammit, she wasn't wrong on any counts. "The good news is, once those things are done, I do think you'll be able to sell the house, and rather quickly at that."

For a tiny fraction of a second, Finn was tempted to say forget it and blow the whole thing off. This house, with its shitty memories, had been sitting here by its lonesome for two years. What did he care if it kept sitting here until it fucking fell down?

But that was the problem. Finn *did* care. He was tired of shitty memories. He'd already put one part of his past behind him in coming to make amends with Asher.

Now he was going to put another part behind him once and for all by selling this house.

"Okay," he said, letting go of the exhale that had been stuck in his throat. "Let's plan on putting this place on the market in three weeks then. I'll get started on the repairs first thing in the morning."

January's eyes flew wide. "You're going to do the work yourself?"

Dana excused herself quietly, the front door giving up a haunted house-style creak and rattle as she stepped onto the porch, leaving Finn to nod.

"Well, I'm not a contractor, so I'm sure I'll have to hire someone to do a lot of the more complicated stuff. But the off-season just started, and all I'm doing is sitting around, waiting for my agent to broker this new deal with the Rage. I've got the time."

Yeah, Finn could go back to New Orleans and spend that time hanging out with his teammates, but most of them were scattered all over the place now that they'd won the Cup. The work here needed to be done. Sticking around for a few weeks wouldn't kill him.

"It's an awful lot to take on," January said, spinning a doubtful gaze over the dust-smudged windows and dinged-up doorframes.

"I know. But what was it you said?" He broke off in a silent rewind, reaching out to slide his hand over hers. "Getting upset is a waste of energy. I've got to do the best I can with what I've got."

Grinning, she laced her fingers through his. "I guess I did say that. Lucky for you, the best you've got includes me. A couple of the guys at Seventeen do licensed contract work on the side. I bet they'll be able to help you out with the bigger jobs pretty fast. And of course, I can help too."

"Really?" Finn asked, surprise tagging him right in the sternum. "It's going to be a ton of work."

"Mmm hmm." January turned, pressing up to her toes to kiss him. "I'm sure you'll find a way to thank me later."

CHAPTER 8

January swung the sledgehammer in her grasp until the deck railing in front of her collapsed with a satisfying crack. Adjusting the safety goggles that both Finn and firefighter-slash-contractor Ryan Dempsey had insisted she wear, she wiped her brow with her forearm as she paused to catch her breath.

"You okay?" Finn asked, walking over from the scrap pile he'd just gathered for the dumpster to pass her a bottle of water from the nearby cooler. "Here. It was hotter than hell's kitchen today."

January squinted at the dusky evening sky, sliding her safety goggles to the top of her head. "Yeah, but I haven't been out here for a full four days like you."

Still, she uncapped the frosty bottle for a nice long draw, because A) she really was thirsty; and B) she also wasn't stupid. She might only be clocking a few fix-it hours after work every night, but she could still wind up with heat exhaustion if she wasn't careful.

Finn lifted a damply T-shirted shoulder, and *God*, she

would never get enough of those muscles, clothed or otherwise. "Ah, the work isn't so bad. Plus, I've had help."

He'd no sooner finished his sentence when Dempsey rounded the corner from the front of the house with a crooked smile on his lips. "Hey. I resemble that remark," the firefighter said cheerfully.

"Yeah, I'm glad you do," Finn countered past his grin. "Because I'd be pretty hosed trying to replace both this deck and the rickety-ass front porch on my own."

"Ah, they're a piece of cake when you've got enough able bodies helping out. Speaking of which"—Dempsey let his bright green stare move over the small, somewhat cleared backyard before turning back to look at Finn—"it's getting late, and you put in a helluva day with getting this yard in shape. Why don't you let me and Gates finish tearing down this railing so you two can get out of here?"

January's brows lifted. "Are you sure?"

"As shooting," Dempsey said with a brotherly wink. "Come on, J. You've been busting your butt on the fundraiser all week, and anyway, your boy here is paying me. The least I can do is spring you both with enough time to have a late meal together."

A flush crept up her cheeks at the more-than-friends implication, but Finn just crossed the grass to shake Ryan's hand like nothing-doing.

"Thanks, man. I appreciate it."

Dempsey laughed, tipping his navy blue RFD baseball hat in Finn's direction. "Don't thank me yet. When we've got the full crew here on Saturday, pizza and beer is on you."

"Just for that, I *am* leaving now," Finn laughed back.

After a round of goodbyes to both Dempsey and one of Seventeen's other rescue squad firefighters, Tyler Gates, January traded in her sledgehammer and safety goggles for the keys to her MINI Cooper. Still slightly sweaty, she slid behind the wheel, trying and failing to hide her smile as Finn origamied his way into the passenger seat.

"Whoever designed this thing definitely didn't have professional athletes in mind," he grumbled. "Or most of the human population, for that matter. Seriously, how are you even a little comfortable right now?"

"Um, because I'm not six three. You could always go back to the car rental agency," she teased. He'd returned the SUV when he'd extended his stay in Remington, grabbing rides to the house every day from either her or one of the guys on Dempsey's crew. "They might have a stretch limo. Or—oooh! A monster truck."

Mischief flickered through Finn's whiskey-colored stare, sending an unexpected and oh-so-delicious shot of heat between January's hips. "Funny. On second thought I'll stick with this. Being in close quarters with you has its advantages." He turned to gesture to her laptop bag, which was stuffed so full, it easily took over more than half the back seat. "Although we're in a little closer than usual tonight. Not that I'm complaining, but…"

Just like that, her smile disappeared and her belly filled with a whole lot of *ugh*. "Sorry. This fundraiser is killing me. It's actually a good thing Dempsey kicked us out, because I've probably got hours of work ahead of me."

"Anything I can help with?" Finn asked, and she shot him a quick, appreciative glance from the driver's seat.

"Not unless you can come up with a theme idea that will make this event a blockbuster, and believe me, I've tried. Casino night, masquerade ball, wine tasting—they're all completely played out."

The face he made told January she'd been right to cross the themes off her list. "Yeah, no offense, but they do sound pretty overdone."

"I know." She blew out a frustrated breath. "The crappy

part is, if I have any prayer of getting the logistics in place, I'm out of time. I guess I'll just have to pick the least boring theme and give it my best shot."

Finn sat back, watching the traffic around them silently for a few minutes before he said, "I know you said the patrons are Remington's elite, but this *is* a fundraiser for firefighters, who are a lot more laid back. So what if you went outside the box for a theme?"

Not wanting to discard anything off the bat, January turned the idea over in her mind before answering. "It would be risky. Yes, the fundraiser is for firefighters, and of course, they all attend to socialize with the donors. But it's always been a formal event."

"Yeah, but it's also a formal event that's losing its effectiveness."

Well, shit. Of course there was that. "True. I'm just not sure what I could come up with that would be different and fun, yet still a big enough draw to appeal to potential donors."

"What about a sports theme?" Finn asked, a slow, sexy grin hanging in the words. "Specifically, oh, I don't know. Hockey?"

Her brows creased in confusion. It wasn't a terrible idea —in fact, it was pretty damned good. Except… "I only know one hockey player."

"Maybe. But I know lots of them."

Shock sent January's heart smacking against her rib cage, excitement kicking it even faster as she pulled over to properly stare at Finn.

"Are you kidding me?"

She heard the gracelessness of the question only once it was out, but Finn just laughed.

"I've spent three years in the league, and four more scratching my way up the ladder to get there. I'm pretty sure

I'm serious about knowing a guy or two...dozen."

"Okay, that was a stupid question. What I meant was, this event is just over three weeks from now," January said, her brain fighting for control over her giddiness as she tried to consider all the variables. "Do you really think your teammates would be willing to drop everything and come out to Remington for a fundraiser?"

Finn shrugged, his T-shirt shushing against the MINI's passenger seat. "Realistically, I'm sure not everyone will be able to make it, but we're in the off-season, remember? A lot of the guys on the Rage are probably at loose ends, and they're always up for a good time. Plus, this is a great cause. I bet if I threw it out there, most of them would be up for it."

Oh God. Oh God, with the draw of a Cup-winning team in attendance, this just might work. "We could go with a whole game day theme. Pennants, trading cards for autographs, the works. And we could make the event really laid back—no tuxedos or fancy dresses, just relaxed, casual fun to set the mood. Team jerseys, jeans, ball caps. Oh!" A fresh thought popped into January's head, and yes! *Perfect*. "What if we organized a silent auction too? That way, even the players who can't make it in person can still donate signed memorabilia or other items if they want to help out."

"That's a great idea," he said. "We do things like that for local charities a lot, so I'm sure you'd get a decent response, even from the guys who can come."

Another wave of ideas burst through her mind, each one building off the one before it. "With a game day theme, we can go low key on catering, which will free up more of the budget for advertising."

"A couple of the guys on the team have pretty big social media followings. I bet you could sweet-talk them into making a post or two for the cause." Finn paused, a tiny frown tugging at the corners of his mouth through the evening shadows. "The only part of this that sucks is that you're still stuck with Chase Manor. The place doesn't exactly scream 'game day.'"

January's brain launched one last idea, and for a second, she nearly balked. She was already taking a risk with this theme. A change in venue—especially *this* change in venue—wouldn't just be risky. It would be downright crazy. But she'd already tried playing it safe for this fundraiser, and the only thing it had gotten her was a bucketful of blah.

Finn was right. The old way wasn't working. If she wanted to change things—if she wanted to raise the money for that fire equipment—she was going to have to go all in.

"Chase Manor might not scream 'game day', but I know a place that does. Can you do me a favor and hand me my cell phone? I've got a call to make."

~

JANUARY WRAPPED her fingers around the handle of a sledge-hammer and swung as hard as she could for the second time in a week. But this time, she had an audience, and striking out in front of every firefighter plus both paramedics at Station Seventeen was *so* not on her agenda.

"Wow. Way to get it done, January!" Dempsey said after the rotted-out section of porch railing fell to the grass below with a heavy thump.

"Remind me not to ever piss you off," added Shae McCullough as she sent a definite look of approval in January's direction from the spot where she stood in the side yard. January was tempted to point out that Shae trained as hard as any of her male engine-mates and could probably out-sledgehammer the hell out of any porch railing on the planet, but before she could say so much as a word, Kennedy stuck her head through one of the wide-open windows on the front of the house.

"Of course January's a badass. Look at the company she keeps. Also—hello—Sarge's daughter."

A chorus of murmured agreement floated through the muggy Saturday morning air, and finally, January laughed. "Okay, okay. While I appreciate the ringing endorsement of my badassery"—she paused for a dusty curtsy on the dustier porch boards—"we have a ton of work to do. If you're not sure what project you're on, there's a clipboard in the kitchen with a detailed list, or you can check in with me or Dempsey, too. And make sure you hydrate! I know Parker and Quinn are paramedics, but don't make them work on their day off."

Everyone in the group scattered to their various posts. Grinning, January turned to pick up her sledgehammer and get to work on the next section of the porch railing, but the sight of Finn, leaning against the front doorframe and giving her a sexy, smirk-filled up and down look, stopped her in her tracks.

"You made a project schedule?" he asked, one shadowy brow lifting toward his just-unkempt-enough-to-be-scorching-hot hairline. The muscles in his shoulders flexed and released beneath his dark gray T-shirt as he straightened to a full stand, and heat flooded through her at the thought of what those shoulders had looked like less than two hours ago when she'd wrapped her arms around them and screamed his name.

Focus. On something other than Finn's insanely sculpted body and all the magical things he can do with it, please and thank you. "Oh! Um, yes," January said blinking herself back to the reality of the front porch. "Dempsey said assignments would be helpful, and these guys are used to that sort of thing from working at Seventeen. Plus, looking at the logistics of each project to determine how much manpower will be needed, then dividing everything up according to experience and each firefighter's preference was easy."

Finn's laughter came out in a soft rumble. "As easy as making up your own filing system? Or single-handedly planning a massive fundraiser? Or—"

"Are you making fun of my organizational skills, Finnegan?" She slid one hand to her denim-clad hip to punctuate the sass in her question, but he shocked the hell out of her by closing the space between them and pulling her against his chest.

"No. I'm thanking you. You rallied all your friends and got them to fork over an entire Saturday to help me fix this place up. Not a lot of people would've done that for me." He stopped. Tipped his head in thought. Amended with, "Okay, no one would've done that for me, especially not with a plate as full as yours is right now. I'm really grateful."

An "oh" crossed her lips, more sigh than actual word. "Well, you're helping me with the fundraiser, too."

Finn shrugged. "I made a suggestion and a couple of phone calls."

"You made a couple dozen phone calls," January corrected. "And you even reached out to the two guys you knew from the minors who play for the Rogues now so we could have some local pros in attendance, *and* add a whole bunch of items for the silent auction."

"Ah, those guys were happy to help the RFD."

She pressed up to the toes of her work boots, brushing a kiss over Finn's lips even though they stood in broad daylight on the porch, where any of the firefighters or contractors could mosey on by and see them. "Yeah, but all of those guys on both the Rage and the Rogues were also happy to help you. The truth is, I never would've come up with the idea for a game night theme or the balls to take the risk for something new if you hadn't encouraged me. If we raise the money for the new equipment—"

"When," Finn insisted, and January gave in with a laugh.

"*When* we raise enough money for the new equipment, it'll be in large part because of you."

Lowering his mouth to hers, he returned her quick kiss with a slower, more seductive version. "Guess we make a decent team, huh?"

"Mmm. Guess so. Too bad we have work to do," she murmured, her knees getting decidedly less sturdy as Finn's lips lingered by her ear.

"Nah." He nipped her earlobe, just hard enough to make her shiver before stepping back from her with a devastatingly sexy half-smile. "It'll motivate me to get things done as fast as possible so we can go back to the Plaza and make *very* good use of those showerheads…especially the detachable one."

January's chin snapped to attention, along with some of her more southerly parts. "What are you waiting for?" she asked, half kidding, half serious as a heart attack. "Hurry up and grab your tool belt so we can knock this porch down as fast as possible, hockey boy!"

Letting her gaze linger on his ass for just a second as he descended the porch boards with a cocky "yes ma'am," January turned back toward the sledgehammer she'd left leaning up against the house.

And let out a yelp of surprise when she came face to grinning face with Kennedy in the window.

"Girl." Her friend's jet black hair swung over the straps of her tank top and her tattooed shoulders as she shook her head, her grin morphing into a laugh. "You two are so frigging cute together, I can't even tease you and enjoy it."

"Eavesdropping isn't polite, you know," January groused,

although the smile poking at the edges of her mouth probably erased any zing the words could've carried.

Not that Kennedy would have been deterred either way. "Okay, first of all, I think we can agree that proper etiquette has never been in my fucking wheelhouse," she said. "Secondly, I can't help what I hear if I'm on paint duty and the window is open."

January folded like a bad hand in a high-stakes poker game. "Fair enough. But what's going on between me and Finn is totally casual. We're far from cute."

"*Au contraire.*" Kennedy pointed her paintbrush at January with a less-than-ladylike snort. "You and Finn are ridiculously cute, and I'm not the only one who thinks so. Shae and Quinn agree. You two are totally the 'it' couple right now."

"You talked about this with Shae and Quinn?" January asked, but only after she'd picked her jaw up off the porch boards. Okay, so she and Finn hadn't been hiding what was going on between them, but that was only because there was nothing serious to hide.

Her expression softening, Kennedy lowered both her paintbrush and her voice. "Only in passing this morning. I didn't realize it would bother you. I mean, you really do seem happy with Finn."

"I am," January said, hearing the words before she'd realized she was going to admit them out loud. "But really, we're not the 'it' couple. We're not *any* sort of couple. It's just some great sex and short-term fun."

"Are you sure?" The question arrived without judgment—Kennedy had never been the type—and for one bold, delicious second, January wanted to say no. They'd spent every possible minute together since his day with the Cup, and each one had made her want the *next* one all the more. But the condo she'd bought last year, the job she worked hard at and loved, the friends and family she loved even more, all of those things were in Remington, where she not only lived, but had wanted to live for her whole life.

Where Finn *hadn't* wanted to live for the last seven years, to the point that he'd come back to cut his last remaining ties once and for all.

"Yes," January said, nodding to hammer the word home. "Finn lives in New Orleans for part of the year, and travels all over the country—not to mention half of Canada—for the other part. And it's definitely no secret that I belong here."

Kennedy looked through the window, her normally tough demeanor whittled down to a tiny, honest smile. "That you do. I couldn't imagine the firehouse or the bar—hell, anyplace in the city without you. Still, that doesn't mean you two couldn't give a long distance thing a go."

January's heart stuttered at the suggestion, but she took a deep breath to wrestle it back in line. She'd known the score ever since Finn had taken her to dinner at La Lumière. Whatever was going on between them was temporary, and she had to be okay with that.

After all, they really were having a great time together, and temporary was better than nothing.

"I don't think so," she said, giving her head a firm shake. "Long-distance relationships rarely work out, and even if this one did, eventually, one of us would have to move to be with the other. Finn's about to sign a new contract which would keep him in New Orleans long-term, and my whole life is here. Keeping things temporary is just for the best."

For a minute that felt ten times as long, Kennedy said nothing, just examining January with a sharp, bright green stare. But just when January was certain Kennedy would push back in that balls-out way of hers, her friend reached down to reclaim her paintbrush with a nod.

"Okay, girlfriend. If you say temporary is for the best, then it must be for the best."

"I do," January answered.

Only the words tasted like a lie.

CHAPTER 9

Finn picked up his glass of whiskey and took a nice, long draw off the rim. He relished the burn as the liquid hit his belly, and thank fuck for good liquor.

"What do you *mean*, Babineaux's still playing hardball?" he grated, pushing up from the sofa to pace a swift circuit through the living room in January's condo. He'd had the place to himself ever since she'd (begrudgingly) left for work five hours ago, which as it turned out was just as well. At least she wasn't here to witness Finn's suddenly surly mood or the rare but warranted day drinking he'd started doing the minute he'd seen Marty's text saying they needed to talk.

"I mean exactly that," Marty said, a surprisingly apologetic tone laced over his answer. "He's been dodging my calls since our last meeting. Although with how quickly we rejected his lowball offer, I can't say I'm all that surprised."

Adrenaline combined with the irritation already free-flowing through Finn's veins, and the combination did nothing to lower his normally stellar blood pressure. "Babineaux has been jerking me around with slow responses and shitty offers for nearly three weeks now, Marty. I'm starting to lose my patience."

"Sadly, kid, I think that's what he wants. Smug son of a bitch," Marty added, showing off some irritation of his own. "But rumor has it that on top of being a sanctimonious prick, he's also not exactly thrilled with your extracurricular work over there in North Carolina."

Finn threw back the rest of the whiskey in his glass, middle of the day be damned. "I'm not exactly wasting my time with a bunch of hookers and blow over here. I spent a couple weeks fixing my old man's house up to put it on the market. The realtor listed the place today, for Chrissake."

With the help of everyone from Station Seventeen, he'd been able to get the repairs done nearly a whole week ahead of schedule. Not that anything Finn did on his own time was any of Babineaux's business—as long as it was legal, anyway.

"Right." Marty cleared his throat. "Actually, I was talking about the fundraiser thing you're doing for the fire department."

Finn laughed for a full five seconds until he realized his agent wasn't sharing the sentiment. "Seriously? Babineuax's got to be a special sort of jackass to take exception to his players doing charity work. Especially on their own time."

"I'm not denying the guy's a douche bag," Marty said. "But from a purely business standpoint...the PR you're doing might be for a good cause, but it's not for a good cause in New Orleans."

Oh for the love of... "These guys are firefighters, Marty. They run into all the places everyone else runs out of, which means they deserve decent gear no matter where they suit up. And anyway, Remington's my hometown."

The silent hum on the other end of the phone line told Finn in no uncertain terms that he wasn't going to like what came next, and Marty's next words definitely held up that end of the bargain.

"Maybe, but it's a hometown you denied even having until a handful of weeks ago, Donnelly. Look, I'm all for this fundraiser. I really am. But you didn't do a breath of PR for the Rage when you had the Cup three weeks ago, and believe me when I tell you, you're the only guy on the team who's kept that thing on the down low. Now you're making news outlets by asking your teammates to participate in a charity event that isn't for the home-team community. On top of the high-dollar deal you're asking for and the fact that Babineaux has decided to dig his heels in…this deal is just a really hard sell right now."

Finn hauled in a deep breath, walking his empty glass to the sink in January's kitchen before trusting himself to answer. "I outscored nearly all the centers in the goddamn league this season, and I haven't even reached my prime. There's no *good* reason for Babineaux to hold out this long on a deal we all know I deserve. Not one."

"That may be true, but it doesn't change the fact that he can, and he is," Marty said quietly. "I know you said you don't want to go this way, but I think we should reconsider a different—"

"No." Okay, so cutting the guy off had been a little harsh, especially since Marty was on Finn's side. But he'd earned this deal in New Orleans. He'd busted his ass for it for three long years.

Unless maybe he wasn't the player he thought he was. The player Asher had thought he was.

"Finn." Despite Marty's still-soft tone, the word brought him back to reality with a startling slap. "You should know that the Charlotte Rogues have made you an offer."

His pulse pounded so hard that for just a second, all he

could hear was the white noise of his blood pressing against his eardrums. "What?"

"I didn't lead with it because the offer isn't as competitive as what you're asking for from the Rage. In fact, it's not even close." Before Finn could argue, or even get in a word edgewise, Marty added, "It's quite a bit more than you're making now, though, and there are some incentive options that could bump the number up significantly."

"Give me facts, Marty. How much are we talking about?"

As soon as Marty answered, Finn wished he hadn't asked.

"No." He jammed a hand through his hair before pacing back over to the sofa. The deal had to be better than that. He'd worked too fucking hard for anything else. "Babineaux's just got his shit in a twist because he hates to lose. Once he sees the great PR this fundraiser will give the Rage as a team and he realizes how big of a hit he'll take without those forty-six goals I scored this season, he'll fold."

"As your agent, I'll do what you tell me to," Marty said, and the lack of hesitation in his voice marked the words as true. "As someone who knows you better than most, I feel compelled to point out that you don't seem unhappy over there in Remington. So I've got to ask. Are you sure this is what you want to do?"

No. Yes. No. Finn looked around January's condo, and for the first time, he wasn't sure of his answer. But Christ, he'd thrown everything he'd had at being the Rage's star center for the last three years. He'd earned every single thing he was asking for.

He had to be the player he thought he was.

"Yes." Finn straightened his spine, his shoulders locking into place. "I'm one hundred percent sure."

But the second he ended the call, he headed for the door.

≈

"Hey, J! I found this guy loitering out front. He says he's with you."

January looked up from the stack of paperwork on her desk, her surprise at Kellan's words quickly turning into a shot of pure happiness at the sight of Finn standing next to him in the space leading in from Station Seventeen's main hallway.

"Hey! Oh my God, what are you doing here?" Work forgotten, she stood to clack-clack her way over the linoleum, giving her next thought an immediate voice. "And more to the point, how did you *get* here?"

"I came to see you," Finn said, hitching one shoulder in a brief shrug before lifting his chin in thanks at Kellan, who gave them both a mock salute before slipping out the door. "Thought I'd work in a run while I was at it."

She realized, just a beat too late, obviously, that Finn was decked out in a snug-fitting compression T-shirt and a pair of basketball shorts, and wait... "My condo is almost eight miles from here and it's got to be, what"—she paused to look at the window behind him, through which the sun was shining like crazy—"ninety-two degrees outside?"

"I don't mind the heat. Anyway, the off-season doesn't last forever. I've got to stay on top of my workouts."

He capped his answer with another shrug, this one even more haphazard than the last, and the gesture stirred something odd in January's gut.

She tipped her head to look at Finn more closely, proceeding with care, but proceeding nonetheless. "That ice time you logged with Alec and Trey at the Rogues' facility yesterday wasn't enough for you?"

After he'd reached out to his old buddies to ask them to attend the fundraiser, they'd been all too happy to invite him out to the Liberty Center for some drills. Three hours' worth, to be exact. The thought of it alone had turned

January's legs into Jell-O, but Finn had been so jacked up afterwards, telling her story after story of the time he'd spent with both guys in the minor leagues and actually admitting that the Rogues' facility was state-of-the-art. The grueling physical exertion hadn't put so much as a dent in his upbeat mood.

Unlike whatever was bothering him now.

"Yesterday's workout was okay, I guess, but I really should be stepping up my game," Finn said with all the enthusiasm one might reserve for a root canal, and yep, her red flags were officially whipping in the wind.

Time to cut to the chase. "Okay, what's bugging you? Because last night you were nine kinds of happy at having finished your dad's house and gotten back on the ice for some practice, and now you look pissed enough to spit venom."

Finn's muscles tensed, his mouth flattening into a hard line before he let out a breath in defeat. "I'm sorry. I'm an ass. I got crappy news from my agent about this new contract, and…I just wanted to come out here and see you. That's all."

January's jaw unhinged. "You ran eight miles because you had a shit day and wanted to see me?"

"When you put it that way it sounds…" He trailed off, a laugh crossing his lips in a soft, self-deprecating huff. "Like the truth. Yeah, I had a shit day and I missed you."

"I missed you too," she said. Now that she heard the words out loud, she realized how much she meant them, and how little time she and Finn had left together before he'd go back to New Orleans, and she didn't think. Just moved.

"What are you doing?" Finn asked, his dark brows creasing in confusion as he stepped back to look at her.

But God, she was so far from being confused. In fact, she was one million percent certain as she walked back to her desk and scooped up her laptop bag from its spot beside her chair.

"I'm taking off early. Now did you want a ride, or are you going to run back to my place and meet me there?"

Finn's surprised nod paved the way for his reply. "Sure. A ride would be great."

Falling into step beside her, he offered up a polite greeting to Captain Bridges as she made triple sure he'd be set for the rest of the afternoon without her, then some decidedly less formal 'see ya later's to all the firefighters and paramedics on A-shift as they made their way out the firehouse door. The drive back to her condo was as swift as it was uneventful, and January grinned as she tossed her keys to the side table and lowered her laptop bag next to them.

"Taking off early feels a little decadent. I like it." She kicked out of her heels, and oooh, even better.

Finn looked at her from a few feet away, his expression impossible to read. "You didn't have to leave work early, you know." Emotion flickered through his stare, gone before she could label it, and something strong and deep and reckless made her close the space between them.

"I do know. But it's Friday afternoon. The fundraiser is a week from tomorrow, and the planning is nearly all done. Plus"—her heart squeezed, but still, she held on to his gaze —"you missed me and I missed you."

"I did miss you," he said, his voice as quiet and rough around the edges as the rest of him.

January reached out, brushing her fingers over his. "Do you want to talk about the phone call with your agent?"

"No." Wrapping his arms around her, he pulled her close, his eyes darkening with enough intensity to send a provocative thrill all the way through her. "I don't want to talk about the phone call with my agent. In fact, I don't want to talk about anything. Right now, all I want is you."

Finn leaned in, pressing his lips over hers. But where most of their other kisses were hard and hot and full of urgency, this one shocked her with its softness. He increased the pressure between their mouths in a slow sweep, tasting and testing as if he wanted to memorize every part of her. His tongue slid over her bottom lip, tracing the sensitive skin there for a long, languid minute before pushing past the threshold of her mouth.

But still, Finn didn't rush. He explored in gentle licks and firmer strokes, finding the corners of her mouth, the spot where her top lip dipped slightly in the center, the very tip of her tongue. Each movement was so focused that January had no choice but to feel it without distraction, until finally, Finn pulled back to look at her.

"I really need a shower," he said apologetically, but rather than stepping back to let him move down the hallway for a lightning-fast date with the spray and the soap, January turned on her heel and led the way to the bathroom.

"What are you doing?" Finn asked, his mahogany-colored brows lifting as she reached past the glass of the shower door to turn the water on.

"Well, I know it's not the Plaza. But I'm pretty sure we'll both fit in here, and since I'm suddenly feeling dirty, I thought we could just shower together."

"Did you." From his stare to his voice, nothing about the words was a question. A shiver rippled over her in response, making her breath catch and her nipples bead beneath her button-down blouse.

"I did."

"Hmm." He moved toward her until less than an arm's length separated their bodies, and oh God, her heart was pounding so fast and so hard, surely Finn heard it. "Well," he said, his gaze raking over her like a touch. "I guess if you're feeling dirty, we should do something about that."

January's fingers trembled with anticipation as she reached up to unbutton her blouse.

Only Finn got there first.

"No." The word pinned her into place, every last part of her aching to be touched. Licked. Taken. Slowly, his hands moved over the buttons, freeing them one by one from their moorings in the pale pink fabric of her top. He let the material hang loosely from her shoulders, but only for a second before sliding it free, then repeating his motions with her skirt.

A sound of approval rode past Finn's lips, primal and hot. "So pretty. Christ, you're so fucking perfect."

January was tempted to laugh at the overstatement. But as his eyes took in every inch of her, from her pale pink bra and panties to the darker pink flush of want on her skin, all she could do was believe him.

"Finnegan."

The whisper seemed to hone his focus. With a few economical moves, her bra and panties found the bath mat beneath her feet, and Finn's arms circled around her rib cage as he kissed her again. January tightened her grasp on his shoulders, her fingers moving over the slippery nylon of his workout gear to create friction with the sexy, corded muscles beneath, and oh God, she couldn't wait. Reaching down low, she gripped the hem of his shirt, pulling it up and over his head.

"*Oh.*" Desire shot through her belly, arrowing a path to her clit. How ironic that he'd been the one to call her perfect when he stood in front of her looking so utterly flawless. His chiseled shoulders led to the flat plane of his chest, his small, flat nipples standing out in relief against smooth skin. The trail of dark hair leading between the sharp, muscular *V* of his hips made January's breath jump in her throat.

The sight of his cock, fully erect and pressing against the

fabric of his shorts? *That* turned her desire into full-blown need.

In as few movements as possible, she removed the rest of Finn's clothes and led him into the shower spray. The water slid over them in a hot, steady stream that heightened her arousal. Curling her fingers over his biceps, January swung him around until his shoulder blades met the tiled side wall of the shower.

"January," he started, his muscles flexing under her fingertips as she reached for the soap and began to slide it over his skin.

"Shh." An odd, empowering rush pulsed through her veins, and she gave up a naughty smile to match it. To her surprise, Finn acquiesced, his stare glinting through the steam as it followed her fingers over his body.

January dropped her chin, watching too. The bubbles built to a quick lather as she washed his body, her hands coasting over first his arms, then his shoulders and chest. Finn let go of a moan when she got to his hips, then another when her fingers spread over his powerfully muscled thighs, but the sound in his throat became a huff of surprise when she wrapped her hands around his waist and turned him to face the shower-slicked tiles.

"Back too," she murmured. Spreading the soap across his shoulders, she worked her way over the back of his body, selfishly cupping the strong, solid curve of his ass before slipping her hands around to the front of his hips.

"Oh, *fuck*." The words fell past Finn's lips with all the reverence of a prayer. "God, baby. Please."

"Just tell me what you want, Finn. Tell me, and I'll do it."

His entire body tensed under her touch. January willed her fingers to stillness on the points of his hip bones, waiting, wanting, until he did what she'd asked.

"I want your hands on my cock. Just like this, so I can watch."

Wetness that had nothing to do with the steam or the shower bloomed between her legs, and she complied in an instant. Pressing her chest against his back, she circled her fingers around his cock, moving them in a slow glide. Finn sucked in a breath, releasing it on a harsh exhale before thrusting his hips in time with the rhythm of her hand. He dipped his chin toward his chest, and even though January couldn't see him watching, the thought of it made her sex clench with need.

"Ah," he grunted, his voice thick with lust. "Like that, yeah. Slow and hard."

She kept to her promise, touching him exactly the way he asked her to, stroking and gripping and pumping until his fingers curled into the shower tiles and he bit out a curse, dark and dangerous.

"Christ, you make me crazy and sane all at once."

At her gasp in reply, Finn's body shifted. "Does that turn you on?" he asked, his back still to her. "Knowing how fucking hot I am for you right now?"

"Yes," January whispered.

"You're wet just thinking about it, aren't you."

It was all statement, but she answered anyway. "Yes."

"Then touch yourself."

The command knocked the breath directly from her lungs. Her shock must have translated, because Finn reached down to grasp the fingers on her free hand, pressing them between her trembling thighs.

"Do it," he said. "Touch that perfect, wet pussy while you stroke my cock. And don't stop until you come."

Pleasure unfolded in January's belly, forbidden and scorching hot, and she didn't hesitate. Parting her feet on the porcelain, she curled her fingers, letting them brush lightly over her sex. Her heart slammed at the barely there contact, her throbbing clit begging for more. But Finn had said not to stop, and oh God, oh *God*, she couldn't deny the truth.

She didn't want to stop. Ever.

"Finn."

Under the circumstances, the single syllable was all she could muster. But it seemed to be everything he wanted, because his cock jerked against the hot press of her hand.

"Yes. Fuck, yes, baby. Let me hear you. Tell me how good it feels."

January did. Unabashedly, she moved her fingers deeper, circling them over her clit in fast, hard sweeps, moaning at every sensation. Pleasure burst through her body, persistent and greedy, but she didn't stop. With one hand working his cock and the other buried where she needed it most, she stroked and rocked and thrust, until finally—finally—the edge of release reared up from the sweet spot between her legs.

"Finn. Oh God, I—"

Her orgasm took hold of everything, crashing into her in breath-grabbing waves. Finn turned, breaking her hold on his body and pressing his hand over hers, holding her close as her release sharpened her moans into cries. The spray of the shower rained down around them both, and finally, after a long, hazy minute, January came back to her mind. Finn let her go, but only to open the shower door and silently guide her out of the water. She didn't argue—didn't care that the water was still running or that they were drenched.

The only thing she cared about was having Finn inside her.

Hard and fast and right this minute.

Finn led her into her room and over to the bed, which was still unmade from this morning. He'd been staying with her for weeks—the expense of the Plaza had seemed dumb when they'd been spending every minute together anyway—and his things mingled in with hers, a T-shirt here, a pair of running shoes there. He stretched over the bed, bringing January with him, and God, his tan skin and sculpted muscles looked so provocatively sexy against her snowy white bedsheets.

"Come here." The demand was soft, but she was helpless against it anyway. She slid beneath Finn's body, his hands bracketing her shoulders and her legs falling open so he could settle himself between them. But rather than grabbing a condom and fucking her senseless like she so desperately wanted him to, he leaned in to kiss her. The brush of his mouth was shockingly gentle, and January's heart tripped in her chest.

Finn kissed her slowly, as if he had all the time in the universe to do nothing else, coaxing her lips apart, laving attention everywhere. His mouth lowered to her neck, to her collarbone and the tops of her breasts, tasting everything. Her nipples hardened, aching for his focus, and *oh*, he didn't disappoint. January gasped as he drew one beaded tip past his lips, swirling and sucking until she was certain she'd die or scream or come right there on the spot. She reached between them, closing her fingers over his cock, her desire spiking at the way his body tightened in response.

"You're so beautiful," he said, his gaze full of intensity as he shifted his body up to look at her. "I should've told you seven years ago. I should've been telling you every day between then and now how fucking gorgeous you are."

January's heart thrummed in time with the heat in her blood. "Show me, Finn. Show me now."

He didn't wait—didn't even seem to think. The briefest of movements had a condom out of her bedside table drawer and in his hand, one more had it in place. Sliding his cock over her folds, he tested her body just once before filling her pussy in one slow, deep stroke.

"Oh *God*." Her voice twined around Finn's, who had uttered the same exact words. Her breath stood still in her throat, her brain racing to keep up with the sensations in her body—the full, sweet pressure between her legs, the involuntary clench of her inner muscles, the slam of her pulse at her throat. Finn withdrew slightly, thrusting back into her with intention, then repeating the motion again and again. January lifted her hips to meet each of his thrusts, rocking against him in return, and together they created a rhythm both carnal and intimate.

Release built at the base of her spine, and when Finn slipped his hand into the slight space between them to bury his thumb against her clit, she was lost. She broke apart beneath him, trembling and thrusting and crying out. Levering his hips against hers until no space remained, he shifted to his knees, wrapping his fingers around her hips and holding her wide as he filled her without remorse. The change in angle drew her orgasm out farther, and with one final, balls-deep thrust, Finn joined her in release.

They lay together for a minute, chests heaving and bodies loose. Eventually, Finn slipped to the bathroom, then came back with a towel for her wet hair. They went through the normal motions of drying off, getting dressed, and padding to the living room to settle in on the couch together. But January didn't feel normal in any way, because she was falling in love with Finn.

And in eight days, he was leaving the place she'd always called home.

CHAPTER 10

Finn sat back on his bar stool, looking out at the Crooked Angel's dining room with an ear-to-ear grin on his face. Although he'd spent most of the day helping with preparations for the fundraiser, seeing the place not just decked out according to theme, but jammed to the rafters with guests, firefighters, and the teammates he hadn't seen for over a month was pretty freaking cool.

Seeing January's face, all lit up and glowing with happiness at the smash-hit success of the event? Now that was priceless.

No, check that. It was *everything*.

Finn's heart sucker punched his sternum before settling into a solid thump-thump-thump against his red and black Rage jersey. He might not have come back to Remington with the intention of doing anything other than tying up loose ends and leaving the place behind, but over the course of the last month, the exact opposite had happened. With each day he'd spent here, he'd grown more and more attached to the city he'd left. To the firefighters and paramedics at Station Seventeen, who had not only been Asher's friends, but his family. To his buddies on the Rogues, who he'd fallen back into step with ease that had bordered on the ridiculous.

To the gorgeous blonde currently wearing his jersey and chatting up some guests across the bar, who had snuck up on him in the mother of all blindsides and stolen his goddamn heart.

"Hey, there's the man of the night! We need to buy you a drink."

The sound of Kellan's voice yanked Finn right back to the bustle of the Crooked Angel, and he turned just in time to hear the guy's lieutenant, Ian Gamble, add a gruff, "Yeah we do. This round's on us."

"You do know it's an open bar, right?" Finn cracked a smile, which the two firefighters returned with ease as they settled over the bar stools. "Anyway, I'm definitely not the man of the night," he added. "If you want to celebrate anyone for pulling this thing together, January's your girl."

Gamble lifted a black brow, grabbing three beers from a passing server who was doling them out from a concessions tray, just like teams did in the stands at their home games. "No, dude. January's *your* girl. And she says this kickass party is all your fault. I'm not inclined to fuck with her."

Coming from the six foot five tattoo-covered former Marine, that was definitely saying something. "Probably smart," Finn agreed. "But she's the one who made all of this happen."

"I've gotta be honest," Kellan said, spinning a gaze over the popcorn stand, the autograph signing booths, and the selfie stations where guests could put on assorted team jerseys or other hockey gear and pose for pictures. "January's always been amazing at stuff like this, but she really outdid herself on this one. Cap just said the RFD is halfway to meeting its fundraising goal, and the event only started an hour ago. Between the rest of the night and the silent auction..."

"Looks like we'll all be in safer gear this year," Gamble finished, and Kellan lifted his beer in salute.

"Seriously. I don't know what we'd do without that woman keeping our sorry asses in line at Seventeen."

"Sorry, am I interrupting some weird manversation over here?" The wry question belonged to a pretty, dark-haired woman in jeans and a Rogues jersey, who didn't make any bones about invading Kellan's personal space for a more-than-friendly kiss.

"Hey, Isabella," Finn said, thankful for the distraction from the sudden pang in his gut. "How's it going? Are you having a good time?"

The detective nodded with enthusiasm. "I'm having a *great* time. I brought everyone from the Thirty-Third with me, including the sergeant—who, by the way, took a raft of crap from the entire intelligence unit for wearing the Rage jersey January sent over. Not that we don't like you, Donnelly." She paused for an apologetic grin. "But we're pretty big on our hometown team."

"Clearly," Gamble added, gesturing to Isabella's blue and white jersey.

Unable to help it, Finn laughed. "No worries. And sending over a Rage jersey for her old man sounds like something January would do."

"Yeah, well proudly wearing it despite getting ribbed into next week is definitely something the sarge would do. He's nothing if not devoted to his daughter's happiness. Those two have always been thick as thieves," Isabella joked, and just like that, the pang in Finn's gut went for a double. The sensation went for broke when January made her way over to their group with a bunch of other firefighters and some of the detectives from the Thirty-Third, her ice-blue eyes bright with excitement and her cheeks flushed to match.

"Hey!" She broke into a smile as she looked at him, and Christ, with her blond hair tied into a ponytail on the crown of her head and his jersey and a pair of jeans shaping her dangerous curves, she was the single most exquisite thing Finn had ever seen.

"Hey," he said, grateful for the length of his own jersey, because living down a public hard-on would be as fun as the fourth circle of hell—especially if any of his teammates happened to walk by. "This place is packed. You've got to have nearly everyone on the invite list in here."

January nodded in agreement. "Ninety-two percent, according to Kennedy. Who's keeping very close track at the door because—"

"Fire code," Kellan and Gamble interrupted simultaneously.

"Exactly," January finished with a laugh. Grabbing a beer and a huge soft pretzel from a passing server, she looked around the crowded dining room-slash-game day arena. "Everyone seems to be loving the more laid-back vibe. The new mayor even came over to tell me how much fun she's having, and her press team tweeted the picture of the two of us with the fundraiser hashtag."

"That's pretty cool," Gamble said. "You're like a local celebrity."

Finn tended to agree, but the assessment only made January laugh louder this time. "Hardly. It's these hockey guys who are the huge draw. The silent auction is doing really well so far, too. There have been a ton of bids on the items donated by both the Rage and the Rogues."

Finn nodded, following her gaze to the display of items set up hall-of-fame style, complete with plaques to describe each piece of memorabilia up for auction. "Good. I know

Ford Callaghan was disappointed he couldn't make it, but he's got a lot of stuff going on in Chicago, where he's from." Finn definitely wasn't the only guy on the Rage whose roots hadn't started in New Orleans. "And of course, our left winger Cooper Banks isn't here because he has the Cup right now. But I'm glad the sticks and jerseys he and Ford signed made it in time for the auction."

Addison Hale, one of Isabella's fellow detectives, arched a dark blond brow over her mischievous stare. "Speaking of your teammates, why don't you give us the rundown, Finn? Some of them look yummy enough to eat with a spoon."

Finn nearly choked on the sip of beer he'd just taken, especially when Shae and Quinn and—*Jesus*—every female in the group including January nodded in agreement.

"Deal," Finn agreed slowly, after his beer and his windpipe had decided to play nicely together. After all, most of his teammates were single. While they'd probably way rather be called a bunch of big, brawling badasses, if any of them had a kink for being considered 'yummy', who was Finn to judge?

"Well, you guys have already met Flynn Kazakov and DC Washington," he said, gesturing to the booths where the Rage's goalie and their dark-haired defenseman—also Finn's two closest friends on the team—sat signing autographs. "And the guy over there talking to January's dad is our new head coach, Mason Courage."

"The woman your coach is chatting up is pretty hot," observed Dempsey from a few bar stools over. "Is she part of the organization too? Because I could get down with an introduction."

Finn snorted. "You could give that a try, but I wouldn't recommend it. That's Juliette Courage. She's a former beauty queen. And oh by the way, she's also the coach's wife."

Dempsey lifted his hands in concession, and a ripple of laughter went through the group. "Okay," Addison said after giving Dempsey a not-small amount of side-eye. "What about that guy over there with the knee brace? He's pretty easy on the eyes. And by 'pretty', I mean 'very'."

"Who, Anders?" Oh hell, this was too good to be true. Not that Finn would tell Addison that there was a hundred and fifty thousand-dollar bounty on the poor guy's virginity. "He's one of our left wingers. He was injured in Game Six, but he's healing up now. You want me to introduce you?"

"Do fish swim? Hell yes I want you to introduce me," she said, and huh, suddenly Dempsey was returning the favor of that side-eye.

Finn turned to January, brushing a kiss over her lips. "I'm going to go hang out with the guys and do some meet and greet with the guests. See if we can't convince more of these people to make a big, fat donation."

She laughed, kissing him right back. "Go. Have fun."

"I will," he said, and making good on the promise wasn't tough. He introduced Addison and Quinn to Anders and their right winger, Ransom Cox, and they traded just enough stories to make for decent laughs but not trouble. Wanting to follow through on his promise to encourage the guests to make donations to the RFD, Finn put on his PR face and worked the room, posing for pictures with Rogues fans as well as his buddies Alec and Trey. About halfway through his circuit around the jam-packed dining room, he caught sight of a man standing a few paces away with a wide-eyed little boy in a Rogues jersey, and after a whispered conversation between the two, the man tentatively approached.

"Sorry to bother you. I'm Rick Gerard, one of the fire-fighters over at Station Six."

"You're not bothering me at all," Finn said, extending a hand toward the guy. "Finn Donnelly. I play center for the Rage."

"Oh, we know." Rick laughed a little, gesturing to the boy,

who was shyly clinging to his hand. "We're really big hockey fans. Anyway, I just wanted to say thanks for supporting the RFD. I'm sure you guys have tons of worthy organizations asking for help. On behalf of my firehouse, we're really grateful you picked ours."

Finn's breath tightened. "It's the least I can do. Believe me." Tilting his head, he bent down to eye level with the boy, draping his forearms over his thighs. "So you're a big hockey fan, huh?"

The little boy nodded. "Y-yes."

Rick squeezed the kid's hand. "This is my son, Jackson."

"Hi Jackson. You must really like the Rogues," Finn said, pointing to the kid's jersey. He paused for a long second before eking out another shy nod, and Finn smiled. "I like the Rogues too."

"You do?" Jackson asked, surprise covering his face.

"Sure. I mean, I play for the Rage, so I also like them a lot. But I'm from Remington, and I have a lot of friends who live here." Finn's eyes darted to the spot where January stood over by Captain Bridges and her father, and man, the words just felt right. "See that lady over there, with the blond hair? She's my very best friend, and she planned this whole party. I wanted to help her, but I also want to help firefighters like your dad, who keep everyone in Remington safe."

Jackson bit his lip and looked at Finn. "So it's okay if I like the Rogues best?"

"Sure, buddy. In fact, have you met Alec Duchene and Trey Parkinson?"

Rick and Jackson traded twin looks of shock. "No," Rick answered, and talk about the biggest no-brainer on the planet.

"Well." Finn pushed to his feet and scanned the dining room, spotting his former teammates over by the selfie station. "Let's fix that. I bet we can get a bunch of pictures and some trading cards for you, too. How does that sound?"

Finn walked them over to Alec and Trey, making introductions and snapping a bunch of photos with Rick's iPhone. Jackson insisted that Finn be in some of the photos too, and saying no to the kid's obvious excitement was a physical impossibility. He posed for selfies and signed fundraiser programs and greeted guests, finally covering the bar from end to end just as Captain Bridges took to the microphone over by the double doors by the Crooked Angel's front entrance.

"May I have your attention please?" he asked, his voice instantly hushing the crowd. "I'd like to thank you all for coming tonight, and for supporting the Remington Fire Department. It's with great pleasure that I announce that as of this moment, we have officially exceeded our fundraising goal."

A huge cheer went up from the crowd, and Finn added his in with a laugh. Not that he'd ever thought they wouldn't raise the money, but damn, the news was good.

"Now," Captain Bridges continued, settling the crowd back into relative quiet. "The truth is, we never would have made it to this point without some incredible hard work and dedication. With that, I'd like to recognize January Sinclair, who organized this event. Please give her a well-deserved round of applause."

Finn's heart pounded with pride as he watched January cross the room to stand by her boss, and Christ, she'd never looked more beautiful.

"Thank you," she said, grinning into the microphone. "I'm thrilled to have exceeded our fundraising goal and know that the men and women of the RFD will be safer as they serve this community that I love so much." A ripple of applause went up, and January waited it out before adding, "However,

I can't take all the thanks. The idea for this fundraiser, along with much of the planning, came from Finn Donnelly. Without him, we wouldn't be here."

January looked at him through the crowd, her blue eyes full of emotion, and even though they were surrounded by hundreds of people, Finn suddenly felt like there was no one else in the entire bar—or hell, maybe even the universe.

"Thank you for having my back," she said.

And in that moment, with every eye in the entire house fixed firmly on him, Finn knew two things. One was that he was insanely, ridiculously, head-over-skates in love with January.

The second was that he was going to take the offer from the Rogues.

~

"This is insane," Finn muttered, tiptoeing (as best a guy his size could, anyway) out of January's bedroom and into her kitchen. They'd gotten back from the fundraiser way too late last night for him to call Marty, and even though the sun was barely coloring the sky with a palette of purple and orange, he couldn't wait any longer.

Insane or not, he needed to make the call, even if it would change the career he'd worked his ass off for.

Flicking his iPad to life, Finn propped it on the counter at the breakfast bar, settling himself onto one of the bar stools there. The call was a big enough deal that he wanted to do it as close to face to face as possible, so he tapped the FaceTime icon, pulled up Marty's smiling face from his list of contacts, adjusting the volume to its lowest feasible setting so he wouldn't wake January as he initiated the call.

"Donnelly," Marty answered on the second ring, and

Christ, the guy really *didn't* ever sleep. "How's my fucking rock star hockey center?"

Finn laughed, albeit quietly. "The Rage strung me along for a goddamn month. I'm good, but I'm not so sure rock star applies."

"I'm gonna have to call you out on that one," Marty said, the cagey excitement in his voice snagging every last ounce of Finn's attention. "Because I just got off the horn with a very contrite Michael Babineaux, and he made you the offer of a lifetime."

Marty followed the news with some numbers so high that Finn actually considered getting dizzy. "Wait, what?" he asked, shock pinning him into place on his bar stool. "He's been holding out forever. What the hell changed his mind?"

"You and that fundraiser, that's what. Jesus, Donnelly, I know you said he'd come to his senses once you showed him some PR, but I have to admit, the whole thing was brilliant."

"The whole thing," Finn said slowly, his brain desperately trying to catch up to the fireworks going on in his rib cage.

"Yes, you sly son of a bitch! Social media practically blew up with pictures of that shindig last night. Some cute blonde wearing your jersey and schmoozing with the mayor, you hamming it up with those guys from the Rogues, and—my personal favorite—the picture with you and that kid. Babineaux couldn't possibly say no to you now without looking like a schmuck and a half, and no way is he going to let you go to the Rogues. Christ, it was a PR *coup*. Of course he fucking called me with the offer."

Finn opened his mouth to tell Marty he had everything dead wrong. Finn hadn't helped January for his own gain. Hell, he'd been fully prepared to take a (far, *far*) lesser deal from the Rogues less than five minutes ago. But before he could loosen the words, realization slammed into him with all the force of a defenseman tearing over the blue line at full speed.

The Rage had made him the offer of a lifetime. The offer he'd wanted.

The offer he deserved.

"What about the Rogues?" Finn asked, and Marty laughed.

"And I thought I was the cutthroat one," Marty joked. Something about Finn's expression must have conveyed that he expected an answer, though, because he continued with, "After last night, they'll probably scrape together all that they can to get you. Buddying up with their two star players was a nice touch, by the way. But there's no way the Rogues will be able to touch the offer Babineaux just made."

Finn's pulse rushed, filling his ears with a roar despite the pin-drop quiet of the kitchen. Yes, Marty was misinterpreting his motivations, and yes again, Finn had spent an incredible month here in Remington. But the truth was, he hadn't even expected to stay longer than a day or two. He'd spent the last three years with the Rage, pouring everything he had into being a part of the team there—of being someone worthy of a championship. He'd done that in New Orleans.

Not Remington.

"Kid?" Marty's voice filtered over the line, his hand waving across the image on Finn's iPad. "You're not having second thoughts, are you? What with Remington being your hometown and all?"

"No," Finn said, resolve forming a cold, steely ball in his gut. "I'm not having second thoughts. I've wanted the deal with the Rage from the get. I don't belong in Remington. I never have. Give me a couple hours to figure out a flight. I'll be back in New Orleans by nightfall."

CHAPTER 11

January stood on the threshold of her living room with her heart in her throat and her hands balled into fists. Okay, so eavesdropping wasn't usually something she'd put on her list of things that were cool to do, but as soon as she'd heard Finn's agent talking about the fundraiser, then the deal from the Rage and the apparent counter-offer from the Rogues, all bets for walking away in the name of privacy had been off.

Just like right now, all bets for keeping her cool were a statistical impossibility.

"Did you use my fundraiser to get a more lucrative job offer?"

Finn's shock showed in only the slightest tightening of his shoulders before he slid from the bar stool to face her. "How long have you been standing there?"

"Long enough." January knotted her arms over the front of the tank top she'd slept in, mostly to cover her slamming heart. God, what an *idiot* she'd been!

Finn hadn't cared about her or the RFD. He'd used her to get what he wanted, and now he was going to leave her behind, just like he had seven years ago. And rather than being once bitten, twice smart-as-hell about it like she damn well should have, she'd gone and fallen in love with him. *Again.*

On second thought, 'idiot' wasn't nearly strong enough.

"This isn't what it sounds like," Finn started, but January cut him off with a barbed-wire laugh.

"Really? Then you didn't just get an offer for an ungodly amount of money—an offer which, oh by the way, you hadn't been able to get all freaking month—because the owner of the Rage caught wind of last night's PR?"

He flinched. "Yes, but—"

Anger sparked and flashed, prompting her to cut him off without regret. "And did you plan to use the RFD fundraiser as leverage in brokering that offer?"

Finn's pause arrowed directly into January's chest. "Okay, yes, but not the way you think."

"Not the way I think?" she asked, and oh, that was priceless. "I realize I was gullible and love struck enough to fall for your I'm-a-better-guy routine all month, but please, do me a favor and stop insulting me now that I know the score."

In an instant, Finn's gaze darkened, and he stepped toward her on the carpet. "You're absolutely right, January. You *do* know the score. We've both known it since I got here. I live in New Orleans, and that's where I belong."

"Do you really believe that?"

Her heart launched the question before her defenses could haul it back. Yes, the realistic part of her had known that Finn was waiting on an offer from the Rage, and that when he got it, he'd be leaving for New Orleans. But the rest of her had seen him become part of the community—part of her community, her family, her life—over the past few weeks, and dammit, Finn belonged there.

Or maybe she'd just foolishly, trustingly, stupidly *wanted* him to belong there, when what he'd wanted was leverage for a killer job offer and a few weeks' worth of no-strings-attached sex.

For a second, Finn said nothing, an odd flare of some unnamed emotion moving through his eyes. But then it was gone, replaced by something cold and lifeless that January had only seen once before.

"Yes. I believe that because it's the truth. This was cool while it lasted, but I belong with my team in New Orleans. Just give me a couple of minutes to get my stuff together, and I'll be out of your hair for good."

～

FINN SAT at the terminal in the Charlotte airport with his duffel bags at his feet and his chest full of nails. Yeah, the second part was metaphorical, and probably a little dramatic on top of it, but still, no matter what Finn thought or did, he couldn't loosen the bone-deep ache that had settled between his ribs.

How had everything he'd ever wanted gone from zero to cluster fuck in the span of one goddamn morning?

"Suck it up, buttercup," Finn grumbled, grateful that his flight didn't leave for another six hours, thus leaving the terminal dead-empty of anyone who might overhear him. His blowout with January might definitely fall under the train wreck category, and the whole nails-in-the-chest thing might largely be grounded in the fact that she (erroneously) thought he'd used her fundraiser entirely for his own gain. But at the end of the day, the truth was still the truth.

He'd wanted the offer from the Rage. Hell, he'd put in enough time, sweat, and energy to earn every penny. He belonged in New Orleans.

Do you really believe that?

The words filtered through Finn's brain, the anger and hope in January's voice as she'd asked him the same question this morning sounding off in his ears, and he stuffed it back, once and for all. He'd come back to Remington to close a chapter in his life that had long since ended. He had the deal he'd worked for, on the team he'd been part of for the last three years.

Leaving now—for good—was his only choice.

Blowing out a breath, Finn pushed to his feet. Sitting here brooding was only going to make him bat-shit crazy, and anyway, he had a ton of time to kill. He might as well grab something to eat to try and kill the ache in his chest.

Fuck, he missed January.

Finn shouldered his bags, focusing on the burn in his muscles as he went to make his way to the main terminal. But before he could get so much as three steps from the gate, his cell phone made a holy racket from the back pocket of his jeans.

"What the hell?" Finn said, his confusion morphing into a quick burst of hope, then a hard shot of dread as he recognized the number on the caller ID. "Kellan?"

"Hey, man," the firefighter answered, his voice serious.

"Is something wrong at the firehouse?" Finn's pulse rattled, and the sensation didn't get any better with the guy's reply.

"You tell me. January showed up about an hour ago even though it's her day off, and she looks like hell in a hand basket. Said you left this morning to go back to New Orleans, and that you're not coming back."

Unease climbed the back of Finn's throat. "Yeah. It's complicated."

"Right." Kellan paused, and Finn could hear the guy measuring his next words in the soft buzz of silence on the line. "Look, I don't know what went down between the two of you, and I may be really out of line for saying this, but that doesn't mean I'm not going to. You're a cool guy, and I appreciate everything you did to help us out. But January's one of us, and over here at Seventeen, we look out for our own."

"I know," Finn said.

"Good. Then you also know she'd do anything for the people she cares about."

Despite the emotions making a spin-cycle out of his gut, Finn's mouth lifted in a smile that was way more irony than joy. "I know that too."

"Then do me a favor and tell me one thing. Why are you wherever you are and not here returning the favor, when the person she obviously cares about above everyone else is you?"

Just like that, all the air funneled from Finn's lungs, shock and sadness and something much, much deeper rooting him to his spot in the empty terminal. He'd been so tangled up trying to move forward, to get ahead and prove his worth, that he hadn't seen the one thing that had been right smack in front of him the whole time.

January *did* care about him. No matter who he played for. No matter how many goals he scored or what sort of deal he got offered. She cared about him enough to make him part of everything she loved.

And he'd gone and fucked it all up by walking out the door. Again.

"You said she's there at Seventeen? Right now?" Finn asked, his heart tripping in his too-tight chest. But he had to make this right. He had to finally be the guy he'd worked so hard to become.

And that guy cared about January above everyone else.

"Yeah," Kellan said, but Finn's feet were already in motion, carrying him to the exit as fast as he could force them to go.

"Good. Just do me a solid and don't let her leave."

Although he didn't think it was possible, Finn ran even faster.

～

AFTER THE TENTH time January tried—and failed—to read the incident report in front of her, she threw in the towel. She shouldn't even be here, she knew, but staying in her condo had driven her crazy. Everywhere she looked, there were memories of Finn—the side of the couch where he sat when they marathoned scary movies, the leftover chili they'd shared earlier that week still sitting in her fridge; hell, even the bar of soap he'd left in his haste to get out of her life still sat in her shower, mocking her with the reminder of its woodsy Finn-like smell. So January had done what any self-respecting, freshly dumped girl would do. She'd thrown on a pair of jeans and thrown herself into work.

God, she was hopeless.

Doing her best to ignore the quaver in her chest that meant tears weren't far behind, she forced herself to pick up the incident report for round eleven. Finn had gotten what he'd wanted. He'd left, and he wasn't coming back. Really, she needed to get on with her life.

Even if what she had wanted the most was for him to want *her*.

"Hey, J. You got a sec?" Kellan poked his head in from the hallway, and January worked up a tiny smile even though the gesture took all of her effort.

"Sure. What's up? Do you guys need more task rotation sheets? I printed some up—"

"No, we're good," he said, stopping her mid-reach. "Actually, I was wondering if you could come take a look at something in the common room for me."

"Oh." Her brows tugged down in concern. "Is everything okay?"

"I think so, but why don't you come tell me?"

January stood, a full dose of what-the-hell-are-you-up-to pinging through her veins. But the sensation pitched to its highest setting when they got to the common room, and every single firefighter and paramedic on A-shift, including Captain Bridges, was standing in the room.

With Finn right in the middle of them.

"What...what the hell are you doing here?" she blurted, barely getting the words past her lips, and Finn broke into a crooked smile.

"Since you really like to ask me that question, I guess I should probably answer it the right way this time. I'm here because I screwed up. I'm here because I need to make things right between us. But mostly, I'm here for you, January."

Oh...God. "You said...this morning on the phone with your agent, you said—"

"I know what I said, and I was wrong." A pained look flickered through Finn's stare, but his eyes never budged from hers. "A lot of what you overheard was out of context. Still, I didn't try hard enough to explain it to you, and I want to do that now, in front of everyone in this room. My agent jumped to a lot of conclusions, but I've set him straight. I participated in the RFD fundraiser for one reason and one reason only, and that reason is you."

January's eyes widened in total shock. "Me," she said slowly.

"You," Finn agreed. "You let me back into your life even though I'd hurt you, and you reminded me what it's like to really belong somewhere. And even though I thought that was in New Orleans, now I know it's not. It's here in Remington, with you. I can't promise that things will always be easy, but I can promise you this. As long as you'll have me, I'll never leave again."

So many emotions filled her brain that for a second, she couldn't even think, let alone breathe or speak. But only one mattered, and it was the one she knew above all the others.

"It's a good thing you want to stick around, because easy or not, I never want to let you go."

January moved toward him at the same time he rushed forward to pull her close, and the room erupted into loud cheers and applause. After a minute or two, the firefighters smartly wandered off to give her and Finn a little privacy, and she pulled back to look at him with a grin.

"That was a pretty bold move you made."

"Not as bold as the deal I signed with the Rogues about twenty minutes ago," he said. "But Remington is where I belong, and I have you to thank for showing me the way. I love you, Calendar Girl."

January pressed up to her tiptoes to kiss him, and in that moment, she knew just where *she* belonged.

"I love you, too, Finnegan. I'm glad you're home."

ALSO BY KIMBERLY KINCAID

Want more stories like DEEP CHECK? Check out these other titles
by Kimberly Kincaid:

The Station Seventeen series:

DEEP TROUBLE

SKIN DEEP

DEEP BURN (available June 2017)

The Cross Creek series:

CROSSING HEARTS

CROSSING THE LINE (available August 2017)

The Line series:

LOVE ON THE LINE

DRAWING THE LINE

OUTSIDE THE LINES

PUSHING THE LINE

(also available as a four-book set digitally)

Standalone stories:

SOMETHING BORROWED

PLAY ME

The Pine Mountain series:

THE SUGAR COOKIE SWEETHEART SWAP

TURN UP THE HEAT

GIMME SOME SUGAR

STIRRING UP TROUBLE

FIRE ME UP

JUST ONE TASTE

ALL WRAPPED UP

The Rescue Squad series:

RECKLESS

FEARLESS

And don't forget to sign up for Kimberly's newsletter at
www.kimberlykincaid.com !

Kimberly Kincaid writes contemporary romance that splits the difference between sexy and sweet and hot and edgy romantic suspense. When she's not sitting cross-legged in an ancient desk chair known as "The Pleather Bomber", she can be found practicing obscene amounts of yoga, whipping up anything from enchiladas to éclairs in her kitchen, or curled up with her nose in a book. Kimberly is a *USA Today* best-selling author and a 2016 and 2015 RWA RITA® finalist and 2014 Bookseller's Best nominee who lives (and writes!) by the mantra that food is love. Kimberly resides in Virginia with her wildly patient husband and their three daughters.

Made in the USA
Lexington, KY
16 February 2018